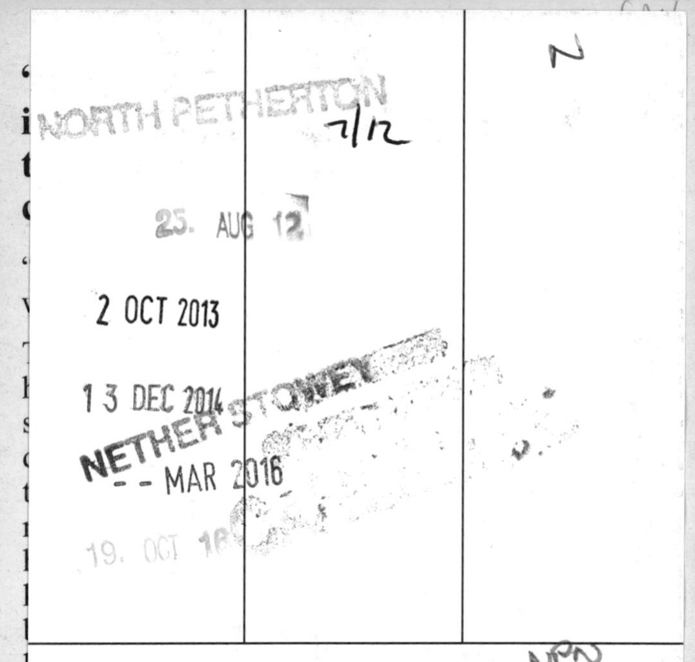

and mouth and t ... else
suffer the conse...

"What consequ... can't
touch me here."

"Can't I?"

Natasha Tate's romantic side has its roots in childhood. Ask anyone and you'll hear she spent too many of her formative years believing she was Cinderella. This despite the fact that she had two loving parents and no evil stepmother in sight. Her earliest drawings were of princess attire, replete with bows, ribbons and multiple flounces, she warbled about her future prince during chores, and began each night by assuming the most earnest Sleeping Beauty pose.

Alas, school did not tolerate such fanciful notions, and she quickly learned to rely on romance novels to satisfy her cravings for happy endings. As an army brat and perennial new kid she consumed a book a day, hiding them within her textbooks while training half an ear on her teachers' lectures. This habit persisted into college, despite her more traditional academic pursuits, equipping her with the skills needed to tame her own alpha male hero.

Now that she's married, and the mother of three strapping sons, Natasha's experiencing her own happily-ever-after. As an author for Harlequin Mills & Boon, she lives her dream of crafting fairytale romances set in modern-day larger-than-life settings. Visit her at www.natashatate.com or e-mail her at natasha@natashatate.com

Recent titles by the same author:

ONCE TOUCHED, NEVER FORGOTTEN
AN INCONVENIENT OBSESSION

FORBIDDEN TO HIS TOUCH

BY

NATASHA TATE

First published in Great Britain 2012
by Mills & Boon, an imprint of Harlequin (UK) Limited.
Harlequin (UK) Limited, Eton House, 18-24 Paradise Road,
Richmond, Surrey TW9 1SR

ISBN: 978 0 263 89041 9

Harlequin (UK) policy is to use papers that are natural, renewable and recyclable products and made from wood grown in sustainable forests. The logging and manufacturing process conform to the legal environmental regulations of the country of origin.

Printed and bound in Spain
by Blackprint CPI, Barcelona

FORBIDDEN TO HIS TOUCH

To my little peanut,
who's all grown up now and off to college.
I'm proud to call you my son.

CHAPTER ONE

"You have to talk to her."

Rafael Chaves looked up from where he crouched over a grapevine to see his employer's normally placid features reddened with anger and distress. Without even asking, Rafael knew the *her* to whom Dante Turino referred. Only one female had the ability to bring the burly patriarch of California's premiere vineyard to such an agitated state.

"About what?"

Turino paced tightly, his boots kicking up dust and his beefy hands clenching fistfuls of sunlit air. "That fool child won't listen to reason!"

Having worked since dawn in the fields, Rafael was tired to the bone and filthy. But no amount of mental or physical fatigue could ever fully distract him from the sweet torture of Sophia's presence in the villa on the hill overlooking the vineyard. He was as aware of her as he was of his own breath, of the rough calluses on his palms, his big, hulking body and its brutal hands that possessed a capacity for violence too terrible to contemplate. "I don't understand," he said in a carefully neutral voice as he slowly straightened.

"She's leaving me. Leaving California. Says she's moving to London and building a life of her own."

Rafael stopped breathing.

Turino blinked furiously, his irritation and frustration stamped upon his features. “She’s already purchased her tickets and is packing her bags as we speak.”

Rafael’s lungs tightened and the heavy thud of his pulse quickened beneath his ribs.

“I forbade her to go. But she claimed she was an adult now and that she didn’t need anyone to take care of her.” Turino’s infuriated expression betrayed how impotent he felt in the face of Sophia’s rebellion. “My Sophia, an adult? She’s just a child!”

The warm scent of soil and ripening grapes filled Rafael’s nostrils as he sucked in a sharp breath and forcibly relaxed his jaw and hands. Sophia had been an adult for a few years now, a fact that continued to haunt Rafael’s thoughts and dreams while escaping her oblivious father’s notice entirely.

Turino spun on his heel to pace a tight circle in the tilled row of black earth, plowing his fingers through his wiry gray hair, while anger at losing his cosseted daughter etched deep grooves from his nose to his mouth. “Why would she do this to me?”

Rafael held himself utterly still, allowing his expression to betray none of his thoughts. “I couldn’t say, sir.”

“Haven’t I given that girl everything?”

Though Rafael knew the question was rhetorical, he also knew the gruff American who’d saved his life so many years ago was blind when it came to his only child. “Of course you have,” he assured Turino. “But you know how Sophia is. Stubborn to the core.”

“I warned her that if she left, she’d no longer be my daughter. That I’d cut her off and never forgive her.”

Rafael was sure Sophia had recognized the truth of her father’s words as easily as he had. “That didn’t change her mind?”

The big man seemed to deflate before Rafael's eyes, his grief already bowing his shoulders. "No. She just frowned in that little way of hers, said she was saddened by my inability to wish her well, and then returned to her packing."

Rafael could see that Sophia's insistence on leaving had wounded Turino more than he cared to admit, and Rafael's inability to ease his mentor's pain sent a flare of distress through his veins. But what could he, a bastard and a nobody, possibly do to help?

"You will change her mind for me, won't you?"

Rafael's stomach clenched at the thought of being close enough to Sophia to try. "I don't think—"

"Please? She'll listen to you."

"No," he blurted, a jolt of panic making the word come out more harshly than he'd intended. "She won't. Not anymore." Sophia had craved his company during the summers of her childhood, when vacations at the vineyard had been the highlight of her year. She'd listened with rapt attention while trailing after him, his world such a marked contrast to the London boarding schools she attended during the year.

She'd even listened to him after her mother's death, when the adjustments of adolescence and grief had cast Rafael in the role of friend, protector and confidant. And he'd allowed her friendship, knowing it kept Sophia from interrupting her busy father with her woes. For years, they'd been inseparable.

Until things between them had irrevocably changed.

Until she'd matured into a woman with ripe curves, golden curls and an intoxicating blend of innocence and sensuality that turned every male head in the valley. Until he'd called a halt to their proximity in order to keep his forbidden longing for her hidden.

"You have to try," Turino insisted, hauling Rafael's thoughts back to the conversation at hand.

Though Rafael didn't ever verbalize his sense of obligation to Turino, they both knew he would do anything for him. *Anything.* But he couldn't risk revealing the way his entire body was attuned to Sophia's slightest movement, how his wretched heart clubbed like a runaway horse whenever she was near. As it was, when he caught so much as a glimpse of her, he felt his tenuous control waver. Weaken. She was far too fine for someone of his debased origins, and he had to remind himself of that fact multiple times each day. Countless times each night. "You overestimate the influence I have over her, sir."

"No. You're the one who underestimates it," Turino snapped, moving forward to grip Rafael's forearm with his thick fingers. "Your opinion matters to her. You know it does. That girl has worshipped you for years."

Torn between the conflicting desire to assist the man to whom he owed everything and the need to maintain a safe distance from Sophia, Rafael fought to deny Turino's request. "It won't work," he claimed. "You know she—"

"If the life you've lived here means anything to you, if *I* mean anything to you," Turino warned, "you'll try. You'll talk to her."

Ten minutes later, Rafael had washed the worst of the dirt and grime from his skin, changed his shirt and climbed the wide steps of the main villa's staircase. He hesitated at the top step, his pulse thundering loudly in his ears while his hands gripped the polished rosewood banister.

He knew from the single time he'd visited Sophia's rooms four years ago, when she'd been ill and asked for him, that her door was the last one on the right. He knew the large, square space was crowded with antique wood furniture, hundreds of books, bright, cheerful rugs and countless yards of white, billowing cotton.

He remembered the way her hair had spread in a gilded fan upon her pillow, the sweet curve of her fevered cheek, the bright blue eyes and the fragile wings of collarbone beneath her long, pale throat. He remembered how small she'd looked in her big white bed and the way her mouth had curved up in an innocent smile when she'd seen his hulking frame at her door.

He remembered, too, the way her guileless expression had changed and shifted, the way she had grown pink and bashful the minute she'd read the hunger in his eyes. It had only taken the one time for her to stop seeing him as the boy her father had saved. One unguarded moment for her to realize that he had become a man.

Glancing at her opened doorway, knowing that she stood mere steps away from his looming presence, every muscle in his body drew taut. His breath thinned and heat coiled in his veins. He stalled, frozen in a purgatory of indecision while his blunt fingernails gouged dents in the banister's polished varnish.

He wasn't certain how long he stood before he braced his shoulders, hauled in a fortifying breath and strode toward the one woman with the power to threaten his control. Stopping at her doorway, he stood in silence for several long moments, watching her as she prepared to leave. He swallowed against a thickened throat while her scent—an intoxicating blend of black currant, citrus and warm cedarwood—robbed him of speech. He'd forgotten how she smelled, had willed his mind to erase the memory of her flushed skin, bright eyes and the cool press of her slim fingers against his rough, hair-dusted arm.

"Sophia."

"Raf," she said without turning. "This is certainly a surprise. Did Papa send you to change my mind?" Her voice, soft and smooth, wound around his chest and tightened. Hard.

"You can't leave like this," Rafael answered as he fought to sound calm. Unaffected.

Separate.

Sophia closed her eyes and inhaled slowly, struggling not to react. Rafael hadn't spoken to her in so long, it took all her strength to continue packing as if his presence didn't affect her. It required all her will to not betray the swell of longing and frustration that collected beneath her skin.

"Did you hear me?" he growled. The bulwark of his tempered anger heated her bowed back and coiled low in her stomach.

"Of course I did." She didn't lift her head, her hands methodical and unhurried as she tucked silk shirts, tailored business suits and toiletries into her bag. "But I don't have time to waste. My flight leaves in less than three hours."

"Exactly. You're being impulsive. Impulsive and irrational, just like always." He strode toward her and she tensed. He didn't touch her, though she could feel his desire to stop her preparations crackling in the slim space of air separating them. It sparked a futile urge to drive him to the point where he'd forfeit his perfect restraint enough to grip her between his big, square palms. To close the distance that yawned between them like some impassable chasm.

She wanted him to touch her, to pull her away from the evidence of her pending departure and demand that she stay. With him. She wanted him to lose control of the emotions that he kept so carefully hidden beneath his beautiful, austere features and let her *in*. But she knew he wouldn't. The past four years had taught her that once he'd made up his mind, there was no changing it. "I'm leaving," she told him. "Whether you agree with my decision or not."

"What are you trying to prove?"

"Prove?" she repeated before straightening and then turning to face him. She abandoned her opened suitcase and strode past him to shut her bedroom door. As much as she knew it unnerved him to be alone with her, she refused to grant him an easy escape. Not when this was her last chance to speak with the man who'd stolen her heart so long ago. "Why don't you tell me, Raf? What do you think I'm trying to prove by abandoning my life, my home and the only real family I have left?"

Rafael didn't visibly react to the closed door or her questions, remaining as still as stone as he tracked her movements. But color rose to darken the crests of his cheeks and his black eyes flashed with an agitation that contrasted with his usual aura of calm control. She was reminded of the ferocious youth her father had saved from the streets, the orphan who'd lived by his wits and will before fate intervened. Before life on the Turino lands had civilized him.

"What? No response?" she asked, coming to a stop before his big, tense body. She hadn't seen him exhibit the snarling emotions of his past for a long, long time, and she knew she was pushing him further than was wise. But desperate times called for desperate measures. "No appeal to my sense of duty, my reason, or my loyalty to a father who's ordered me to stay?"

He merely glared at her, his jaw clenched tight while his stony expression concealed any hint of soft emotion. The hard exotic lines of his Brazilian features and the cold, immutable control he exerted made her long for the days of their youth, when he hadn't minded being alone with her. Before he had become so closed off all the time.

"Since you seem to be as silent as ever on the subject, I'll tell you," she said while her pulse beat uncomfortably against her throat. "I can't keep living like some fragile doll destined to spend her days boxed up and on display. Between you and Papa, I'm always held at arm's length, protected from every risk, and hemmed in no matter which way I turn. I can't live that way."

"Of course you can."

"No. I can't. Not anymore. I need to make my own choices. Take my own chances. I need a life of my own, and I can't have it here."

He scowled. "You have a life others only dream about, and you want to throw it all away for no reason. None."

"I need more."

"More? You already possess unimaginable wealth and the lavish attention of a father who treats you like a princess. What more could you possibly need?"

You. "My freedom."

"Your freedom?" he repeated with a low growl. "You know damn well you can do anything, have anything, your little heart desires. You're just being stubborn to make your point."

"Like you're one to talk?"

His nostrils flared and his fists tightened into knots. "You're going to get hurt."

I'm already hurt. "By whom?" She scoffed audibly, refusing to back down. "London is perfectly safe, even if Mother is gone now. I have both a job and an apartment waiting for me, and I'll be living in the middle of a very respectable neighborhood."

"A big city is more dangerous than the home you have here, no matter where you live. And if it's a job you want, you can find one in California just as easily as in London. There's no need to go overseas."

"I wish that were true."

"It is."

"It's not." No matter what other strategies she'd tried, she couldn't eradicate the barriers between them. He held himself separate. Apart. And always, always alone. Though they'd known each other since she was eleven years old, he'd never allowed himself to play any role but protector.

She wanted more from her life and she wanted more from him. And she suspected he knew it, too. But he'd met her every overture with an impenetrable wall of resistance. He refused to see beyond his obligation to her father, and fought to maintain the distance between them despite the emotions she could sense between his steely surface. She wanted him to admit that she meant more to him than a child he'd vowed to protect, to acknowledge the woman she'd become. And until he did, it was too painful to remain.

"I can't stay here any longer." She looked up into his hard black eyes, willing him to understand. To say the only thing that would change her mind. "But I'll be safe," she assured him. "I promise. You don't need to worry about me anymore."

He ignored her reference to the boundaries of their relationship while the brutal curve of his mouth flattened into a harsh, implacable line. "Your father will never forgive you if you insist on this madness."

It was a price she had to pay, a price that made her stomach tense and her eyes sting. "You're wrong," she said, willing herself to believe it. "He's just angry right now."

"He's more than angry. He's furious. And if you insist on closing this door, it may never be opened again."

Staring at Rafael now, at the harsh slash of brow, the thick, black hair as shiny as a crow's wing and the glittering eyes demanding that she obey, she felt a familiar pang of despair. Of anguish no one but he could ease. The thought of leaving him, of living a life without him, made her want to weep. To scream. To beat her frustrations out against his granite chest until he drew her close and kissed her into silence. Knowing that he wouldn't touch her no matter what she did, that he'd allow other women to share his bed while denying her, made a bleak, impotent anger well up from deep within. "Papa still believes I'm a child," she said, lifting her chin. "As do you. But you're wrong. I've made my decision. I'm leaving."

"And what happens when you get hurt?"

"I won't. I'm perfectly capable of taking care of myse—"

"No, you're not," he snapped. "You're a fool if you think you know the first thing about the world, about all the things that could happen if I'm not there to—"

He cut himself off.

But Sophia heard the panic tainting the edges of his words, panic that infused her with the faintest sliver of hope.

It was a hope she knew better than to entertain, but she felt it nonetheless. Her pulse kicked and a twist of nervousness knotted in her belly. Perhaps it wasn't too late. Knowing how his rejection would flay her, but compelled to risk it regardless, she swallowed hard and forced her fears aside. "Raf..." Nerves paralyzed her throat for a moment, but she forged ahead despite the danger. "If you don't want me to leave, then convince me to stay."

His black gaze sharpened. "How?"

Several tense seconds ticked by while she gathered her faltering courage. "Tell me..." The urge to drop her gaze, to withdraw before he could hurt her, sent a torrent of second thoughts through her head. But this could prove to be her last chance. Her only chance to reverse the path she'd embarked upon. So she summoned her strength and began anew. "Tell me there's a future for us, and I'll stay."

The color leached from his dark face while his sharp inhale rent the air like the lash of a whip.

Despair mingled with her hope while she held her breath and waited for his response.

"Soph…you know I care for—"

"No," she interrupted, a note of desperation entering her voice while white-hot pain lanced her chest. "I don't want you to *care* for me like some annoying little child. Like some pathetic obligation to the man who took you in." She pressed her hands against her abdomen, the need to feel his skin against hers so strong it made her throat contract painfully. "I want you to *love* me. *Me.* As a woman. Just once, I want to believe that—"

"No," he groaned, retreating a step.

She followed, hating that she'd stooped to begging, but in too deep to stop now. "Why?" She reached for him, for the thick brown forearm beneath his rolled, white sleeve. The warmth of his flesh scorched her fingers and she felt his muscles contract to hard, ropy knots beneath her touch. "Why do you always fight me on this? When you and I both know there's something between us, something you refuse to—"

"There's nothing between us." He flung her hand aside, his broad shoulders bracing and his chest moving with his labored breathing. *"Nothing."*

"You're wrong." Her heart quailed as she stepped into his space yet again. "You're just too stubborn and afraid to admit it."

"I'm not." He glared at her, the beat of his pulse visible in the side of his neck.

"I love you," she confessed miserably as she lifted tentative fingers to splay against his sternum and the rapid thrum of his heart. "I've loved you from the moment Papa brought you here and if you'd let me, I'd show you how much. I'd give you anything you want, take everything you wanted to give—"

"Don't." A strong grip against her shoulders pressed her away from him. Heat seeped from the fingers that dug into her flesh and then he snatched his hands back, as if he couldn't bear the contact any longer. "You don't know what you're saying."

"Yes, I do," she insisted, stepping close yet again and wrapping her arms around his wide torso. Desperately, she pressed herself against him, the aching need to touch him overriding her fear of his rejection. Tears burned the back of her nose, blurring her eyes and hitching hard in her lungs as she choked out, "I've let you push me away for four years, and I can't do it anymore. That's the only reason I'm leaving, the only reason I can't stay. I can't pretend I feel nothing when it's eating me up inside and you won't even—"

"Pare de falar," he growled, his hands like manacles of iron as he gripped her face between his palms and pressed her back.

"No," she cried as her hands lost their grip upon his ribs and then rose to curve tightly around his rock-hard triceps. "I won't be quiet just because you don't want to hear the truth. I can't pretend anymore when all it does is make me ache inside. I won't. I've spent half my life wanting you to notice me and this is my last—"

He silenced her the only way he could, by covering her lips with his own and catching her protest with his mouth. She gasped and went utterly still, absorbing the shock of his warm mouth against hers. A firestorm of sensations winnowed through her: the heat of his breath against her cheek, the cradle of his palms against the sides of her head, the slamming heartbeat she could feel in every cell of her body. For a breathless moment, they remained frozen, too electrified to move. But then heat and longing and desire sparked into flame and they both became lost in a torrent of hungry need.

Like starved beasts who've been too long denied, they fed upon each other, a flurry of hands and kisses and frantic, exploring touches. She arched against him, craving him, wanting *everything,* and he pulled her to her toes with a low, primal growl.

She felt the wide possession of his hand against her spine, drawing her up tight against his groin, and she shivered, her senses starved for his powerful weight atop her, his hands exploring, his stretch of burnished skin hot and naked upon her own. His tongue slid along the seam of her mouth and she opened to him, meeting the silk of his wet heat with her own. A tremor caught his limbs and he shook between her palms, his head bent low over her tipped face. She could taste his savage hunger, the brutal need for completion. And she wanted to give it… She wanted… Oh…

Thoughts fled as his mouth devoured hers with rough, drugging strokes. Weakness and longing and pleasure flooded her veins as she whimpered and moved even closer. She clutched at his head, her fingers caught in the cool silk of his hair as she angled her mouth beneath his and pressed her aching breasts up against his chest.

Low against her belly, she felt the tight force of his groin against hers, the banked hint of rhythm as he fed upon her mouth. Wanting him, wanting more, she reached trembling fingers between their fused hips to cup the rigid length of his arousal.

He jerked against her palm, and an agonized groan caught low in his throat as he ripped his mouth free. His hand caught hers, and for one scorching moment, he imprisoned it against his burning flesh while his neck arched and he gasped for breath. She felt the throbbing evidence of his desire, the taut, burning heat against her palm, and whispered, "Make love to me, Raf.... Please. I can't bear it any longer." She twisted her free hand in his shirt and stretched to taste the scented wedge of skin at his throat. "Take me...please. I want this. I want you. I—"

A curse rent the air as Raf shoved her away, pushing her onto her heels and ripping his hands from her shoulders. His chest moved unevenly as he grappled for breath, his nostrils flaring and his muscles taut as he backed away from her.

She stepped toward him, one hand outstretched. "Raf—"

"Don't touch me," he spat with such venom that she flinched.

Silence, broken only by the furious agitation of their breaths, beat the air between them as he glared at her.

Rafael spoke first, his words thick with fury and loathing. "We can't ever do that again," he stormed, and she couldn't tell if he targeted the edict at himself or at her.

Emboldened by his kiss, by the proof of his desire for her, she spoke softly. "Because of what Papa might think?"

"Because of what *you* might think," he boomed. "I refuse to mislead you."

Stiffening as if he'd slapped her, her chest tightened painfully. "Mislead me?" she breathed despite the sting of his rejection. "I'm not misled. What you feel about me is undeniably clear. I *felt* the evidence of it against my hand."

His eyes flashed while his mouth twisted in disgust. "It's clear what my *body* feels. Don't confuse a physical response with an emotional one."

The harsh words and the twist of pain that accompanied them lent a sharp, incensed edge to her voice. "Why? Because you're incapable of feeling anything beyond your loyalty to my father?"

"No. Because you refuse to admit the truth," he answered stonily. "You only see what you want to see and hear what you wish to hear. I'd respond the same way to any woman reckless enough to rub herself up against me."

A stunned gasp iced her chest, his claim flaying her with its brutality. "You're lying," she accused. "I know you feel something for me, separate and above what you'd feel for some random female who happened to *rub* against you."

A muscle flexed in his jaw. "Don't delude yourself. I feel for you the same way I'd feel for any daughter of Turino's. No more. No less."

Ten years of loving him, of watching him as he navigated his way through the strange world that contrasted so sharply with the one he'd known, told her he lied. Nothing he said would convince her otherwise. But she'd wasted enough time trying to get him to admit the truth. And at least his rejection, as agonizing as it was, solidified her decision to leave. "Thank you, then, for clarifying things for me," she said, her taut, indignant tone somehow moving past the knot of pain in her throat. She'd nurse her wounds and weep in private. Later. "I'd hate to leave with my childish misconceptions intact."

He scowled, his anger darkening his expression. "Don't be so dramatic," he said. "There's no need to run away to London just because—"

"Don't you *dare* tell me I'm being dramatic," she said in a tight voice. "You know what will keep me here. If you aren't willing to give it to me, we have nothing else to discuss."

"Then I'll leave," he offered. "This is your home, not

mine. You stay and I'll go. You'll never have to see me again."

"You don't get it, do you?" she cried, her tears so close to the surface she could taste their salt at the back of her throat. "My home, this place, it *is* you. And if you don't want me, I can't stay. Whether you're here or not is immaterial."

"But your father's here," he reminded her in a grim, unyielding tone. "Your life is here. It'll crucify him to have you gone."

"Then stay and help him cope with the loss. You're the one crippled by obligation, not I." She returned to her suitcase and flung the rest of her belongings inside. After she'd yanked the zipper closed, she stood with her back to him and forced her breathing to calm. Somehow, she managed to control the trembling of her hands.

When the air became charged, weighted with unspoken emotion and her decimated hopes, she closed her eyes and held her breath until the door opened and then quietly clicked closed.

Bracing her arms against her suitcase, she blinked to dispel the terrible, torturous memory of his hands on her, his mouth branding hers. She could still feel the hard shape of his arousal against her palm, still smell the scent of his skin. Her flesh tingled, the band of muscles along her stomach refused to relax, and her rejected love lodged like a fist in the center of her chest.

A sob caught in her throat and she choked it back, swallowing convulsively while she clutched the sides of her suitcase with white-tipped fingers. Several torturous minutes later, after she'd battled the urge to curl up on the floor and never rise again, she inhaled, relaxed her hands and straightened to collect her travel documents and purse.

At least you know now.

Slinging her purse over her shoulder, she swiped a knuckle under her eyes to dispel any lingering hint of tears, pulled her suitcase from the bed and then left to claim a life that contained no trace, however small, of Rafael Chaves.

CHAPTER TWO

IT TOOK a tragedy to bring it about, but seven years later, Sophia finally returned home.

Her dear friend and colleague Alexander Bennett had accompanied her on the long trip from London, offering his quiet support while they spent countless hours in crowded airplanes and packed airports. Now, they finally stood in the Sacramento airport terminal at the baggage claim, awaiting the arrival of their luggage.

Sophia felt Alexander's warm regard against her profile before he asked, "Are you okay?"

"No," she confessed. "I feel guilty and wretched and sad and mad and everything in between. I hate this and I'm angry at my father for dying before we had a chance to make things right."

He reached for her shoulder and offered a supportive squeeze. "Is there anything I can do to help?"

Knowing that her dreams of an eventual reconciliation with her father were now impossible, she bit her lip and blinked away the fresh sting of tears. "No."

"Don't beat yourself up over this, Soph. You did everything you could to make amends. He was the one who refused to meet you halfway."

"I know." She did. Seven years of refused phone calls, returned letters and blocked emails had taught her that she'd never get what she wanted. Her father was incapable of forgiveness. Of love. She should have accepted it. Moved on. But she hadn't. She'd kept beating herself against the implacable wall of his rejection, kept nursing the twist of guilt that never strayed far from her gut. "That's the problem. And now it's too late. I'll never know if he'd have eventually forgiven me."

"Yes. But at least you'll have some closure, right?" His sympathetic gaze searched hers. "You'll be able to move on."

"I hope you're right," she told him.

"I am." His warm smile eased the tightness in her chest. A bit. "And if I'm not, we'll go to the local pub and toast our orphaned status together."

"I'm planning on that regardless," she said. "By three p.m., I'll be drunk on Turino wine, courtesy of my father. He'd be so proud," she finished on a bitter note.

His soft blue eyes searched hers. "Are you sure you don't want to just stay with me until the funeral tomorrow?"

She shook her head. "I need to go home, even if it's just to say my final goodbyes. I've been avoiding it for far too long."

"And if they send you away?"

"I'm family. Estranged or not, they can cope with my presence for one night."

"You know I'll be here if they don't, right?"

"Yes." She mustered a wan smile and reached to squeeze his wrist. "Thank you. I don't know how I'd have made it through the past few days without you."

"No thanks necessary." His gaze intensified and his fingers closed over her hand, squeezing tight. "You know I'd do anything to help you, Sophia."

Biting her lip, she dropped her gaze and gingerly withdrew her hand from beneath his. “I know.”

Full night had already settled over the Turino vineyards by the time Sophia arrived. Alone. Though the prospect of returning to the home she’d left so long ago struck panic into her heart, she knew she had to face her past, no matter how awkward and painful it might prove to be. Now, with Papa gone, she had to say her final goodbyes before she left California forever.

Inhaling deeply, she took a moment to gather her courage and survey the Turinos’ ancestral property. Twilight cast the east field, laden with ripe blues and purples in preparation for harvest, in scented silence. The vineyard had grown in size and scope, and the shadowed evidence of new outbuildings, new equipment and Rafael’s impact on Papa’s vision was unmistakable. Seeing the touch of his influence made her pulse throb uncomfortably beneath the surface of her skin and her nerves skitter along her veins. Whatever would she say to him when she saw him again? What would he say to her?

She wasn’t foolish enough to think she could escape to London without seeing him again. Without talking to him. And the prospect of facing him after all this time made her stomach clench with worry and apprehension.

Which made no sense, considering the fact that she was over him and had been for years.

Seven years, in fact.

Rafael hated her. She’d stopped deluding herself about his feelings toward her a long, long time ago. Whether he would welcome her or not couldn’t matter. She had a right to attend her father’s funeral, no matter who disapproved. For twenty-four hours, she was here. And whoever didn’t like her unexpected appearance would just have to deal with it.

Even so, it didn't make it any easier to knock on the tall dark door that separated the woman she now was from the girl she'd once been.

For several long, tense moments, Sophia wondered if anyone was home. But then the front door was pulled open and a trapezoid of yellow light spilled out onto the tiled terrace. Dolores, the aging housekeeper of Sophia's youth, looked the same as always, her thick gray braid draped over one rounded shoulder and her robe cinched high over an ample waist. Her mouth dropped open while her reddened hands flew to her bowed cheeks. "Sophia?" she asked as she rushed out to draw Sophia into a tight, warm hug. "Why didn't you tell us you were coming?"

"You know why," Sophia said, returning her former housekeeper's unexpected embrace while tears rose to blur her vision. Blinking fiercely, Sophia withdrew enough to stare into Dolores's lined face. "I heard about Papa."

"Oh, Sophia," Dolores said as her big brown eyes shimmered with a bright sheen of tears. "It's just awful. Terrible. His passing was so unexpected."

Guilt cinched Sophia's lungs and tightened her throat. "I came as soon as I—"

"Of course you did," she said, lifting both chapped hands to cup Sophia's face. "You're a good daughter."

Sophia's heart contracted with a sharp pang. "You don't have to lie to me. You and I both know Papa wouldn't have wanted me here."

"The man was a fool, God rest his soul. The stubborn brute should have forgiven you eons ago, and I will never understand why he held on to his anger for so long."

Sophia knew her father had never seen her as anything but his little princess, a child to be coddled and spoiled.

Having her grow up had never been part of his plans, and the fact that she'd left against his wishes was a betrayal he'd never been able to forget. Or forgive. "At least Raf didn't disappoint him," she offered quietly. "Papa died feeling proud of *someone*."

"I suppose," Dolores said cryptically as she turned to enter the villa.

"You suppose?" Sophia asked as she stepped over the threshold. She scarcely noticed the mansion's cathedral ceilings, stained glass and imported Italian frescos, hurrying after the housekeeper with her suitcase bumping against her heels. "But I thought since taking Rafael on as a partner, Papa's business has more than tripled its production."

"It has," Dolores said as she avoided Sophia's eyes. "That boy has done wonders with the business, and your father made an excellent choice having him as a partner."

From what Sophia had read in the recent tabloids covering her father's unexpected heart attack, the partnership between her father and Rafael had done more than just make them money. Rafael had become the son her father had never had, the obedient, respectful progeny she could never be.

She'd told herself she was glad.

For both of them.

Except now, she couldn't rid her mind of the photo she'd seen of Rafael while standing in line at the market. He'd been leaving the hospital, his tortured, grief-filled expression slipping past his normal control as he'd flung up an arm to block the paparazzi's cameras. He'd looked so stricken and raw, she'd felt an unwelcome compulsion to soothe his grief, to offer him comfort and solace when she knew he'd never accept it from her.

"Does Rafael feel guilty about what happened to Papa?" she asked. "Did they have a falling-out of some kind?"

"Oh, heavens, no," Dolores said, waving away the suggestion. "Nothing like that."

"Papa wasn't upset that Rafael bought his own land, was he?"

"No, no. Of course not. Having Raf on the adjacent property just expanded things for them both."

"Then what?"

Dolores flattened her lips into a tight seam and exhaled noisily. "It's nothing. I'm just getting maudlin in my old age. Your father loved that boy. And you're right about Raf. He's been good for this place. And he was good for your father."

"But?" Sophia persisted.

Dolores hesitated, opened her mouth as if to speak, and then closed it again.

"Tell me."

Her dark brown gaze returned to Sophia's face. "As good as the partnership was for your father, I'm not sure it's been good for Rafael. He's…well, he's not the boy you once knew," she said. "The last seven years have changed him."

"How?"

"He's…harder somehow."

Sophia's heartbeat increased its pace, knocking uncomfortably against her ribs. "But I thought he's become an unrivaled success. He's supposed to be a veritable wizard with agriculture, finances and marketing. And what about the new winery model he developed? I read it's turned the winery world on its head."

"True. But all that success and money and fame…it hasn't made him happy. Working with your father, living to pay off a debt that he believes can't ever be paid…it's made him harder than he used to be. Reminds me of when your father first brought him here, when he was so angry and defensive all the time."

"It can't be that bad or the business would suffer."

"True. But you know Rafael. He knows how to keep his feelings hidden. He's good at acting civilized when he's not. And he's gotten even better at saying the right things." Dolores pursed her lips and shook her head. "It's only those of us who know him who can see how angry he is."

"Angry? What on earth for?" From all Sophia had heard about the wealthy, handsome and elusive Rafael Chaves, his grasp of business and the intricacies of wine-making surpassed everyone's expectations. He was reputed to be equally comfortable in the fields or in a boardroom, effortlessly gaining the respect of vineyard workers and businessmen alike. "He's achieved remarkable success by anyone's standards and he made Papa proud in a way no one else could. I thought that was all that mattered to him."

"I would have thought that, too. But he's not happy and I tell you, it just breaks my heart to see him so…" She paused and pressed her lips together again.

"To see him so…?"

"Listen to me blathering on," Dolores said, waving her hand between them. "You'll see him for yourself soon enough. Maybe you'll even be able to figure out what's wrong and bring him back to himself."

"Me?" Lingering traces of embarrassment brought a knot of denial to her heart. "I wouldn't count on it. Raf has forgotten I even exist."

"Forgotten you exist?" Dolores repeated while her brow furrowed in rebuttal. "You couldn't be more wrong, child. The only time he shows interest in anything is when I mention you. Unlike your bullheaded father, Raf stops *everything* to listen to news of you."

Sophia shook her head, unconvinced. "He's just being polite. Trust me."

"Why would you say such a thing?" Dolores asked, her eyes clouded with confusion. "You two were the best of friends for years. You're his family."

She had been. But then she'd changed the rules. She'd thrown herself at him, offered him her whole heart, and been thoroughly, coldly rejected because of it. He'd walked out her door and never once looked back. Not once. Seven years of no contact from the silent, uncompromising brute had taught her very well what he truly felt for her.

He felt nothing. She wasn't sure he ever had.

Revisiting the realization now, when she already felt guilty and agitated, only made things worse. "Can we talk about this later? I've been in airports since yesterday morning and I'm—"

"Of course," the housekeeper interrupted. "You must be exhausted. Come," she said, reaching for Sophia's suitcase and bustling down the tiled hallway toward the staircase. "I'll fetch clean bedding for your room."

Despite her fatigue, sleep eluded Sophia. The sounds and scents of home reminded her too keenly of what she'd left behind, of the pointless dreams and hopes that she'd put to rest so long ago. Several hours before dawn, she finally admitted defeat and left the high four-poster bed she'd claimed for the first twenty-one years of her life. Moonlight streamed into her bedroom through her opened windows, painting a lattice of silver on her rumpled white bedspread, her bare feet and the scattering of soft rugs strewn over the dark walnut floor.

On the left, her suitcase lay open, its contents in rumpled disarray. She'd packed in a rush, and hadn't thought to bring a robe. So it was with a hint of trepidation that she strode to the closet she hadn't opened since bidding her past goodbye. She stood for a moment, thinking of how cavalierly she'd left everything behind, and how angry her father had been with her defection.

Expecting her belongings to have been discarded as an unwanted reminder of her existence, she was shocked to discover her entire abandoned wardrobe still intact. Papa had kept her things, despite his claim that she was no longer his daughter. Designer clothes in their see-through garment bags, boxes of shoes in every style and hue and enough accessories to suit any mood crowded the racks and shelves. Stunned, she sank back against the molding, the marked contrast between the functional wardrobe of her present with the lavish extravagance of her past making her senses reel.

She opened one cedar-lined drawer and pulled out the buried ivory silk dressing gown she'd secretly bought with her twenty-first birthday money. She'd felt so grown-up in the beautiful wrap, its style so different from the flannel and cotton of her childhood. Now, she slipped it over her white T-shirt and gray drawstring shorts, savoring the comforting sensation of cool silk over bare legs.

Easing her bedroom door open, she peered out into the hallway. Just like every night of her childhood and adolescence, sconces of faint light cast shadows on the wooden plank floor and drew patterns on the stuccoed walls. Sophia could hear the subtle creaking sounds of the house as the night's gentle breeze buffeted its stone walls. The earthy scents of soil and weighted grapevines filtered through the opened windows at each end of the long hall, reminding Sophia of the countless nights she'd snuck out to play hide-and-seek with Rafael.

Silently, she made her way downstairs, wandering aimlessly through the lower floor of the house that had changed so little in her absence. After a few moments, her fingertips tracked the transition from white stucco to walnut molding at the doorway of her father's office.

Her papa's office had been a sanctuary of male business pursuits, the only room to which he had restricted her access. But she supposed it made sense to go there now, to reacquaint herself with the father she'd never really known. She stepped over the threshold and rounded the door that had been left slightly ajar. A small desk lamp was still on, casting shadows atop the dark desk and the edges of an open ledger. Then she lifted her gaze, and froze as recognition winnowed through her.

Her stomach dove and every muscle went taut. Time slowed, each thudding beat of her heart taking an eon to complete. She must have gasped, but she didn't hear the betraying sound over the thundering of her pulse. For several timeless moments, she simply stood immobile, her nerves strung tight.

What was *he* doing here?

She'd forgotten how beautiful Rafael was, how just looking at his splayed thighs, his big, square hands and the thick column of his neck could make her entire body go hot.

The rhythmic motion of his ribs told her he slept, his head canted against the back of her father's chair and the large account book propped atop his thighs and against the desk before him. After a blindingly long stretch of time, she finally recovered enough to move. Gripping her arms around her waist, she soundlessly crept toward him, tremulous nerves making her breath unsteady and thin.

He was bigger and leaner than she remembered, the hard lines of his chest and shoulder imposing even in repose. He wore a white shirt, open at the neck, and her stomach clenched at the memory of all his smooth, taut skin stretched over laboring muscles as he toiled in the sun. A startling desire to touch him, to press a fingertip to the shadowed dip beneath his throat and then trail up to the scented space beneath his perfectly curved ear, tore through her.

How could he still affect her this way, when it was obvious that time had altered the man she'd once loved, and not in a good way? Yes, he still possessed the same sensual mouth, the same austere jaw and brow, the same sweep of black, curling lashes. But the scowl that had so often claimed his expression before she left had become permanent, its lines of bitterness and anger etched into his features like seams within a stone.

Oh, Raf, she mourned, *why must you always be so unhappy?* Helpless to stop herself, she inched closer, the old, futile desire to bring him peace churning deep in her gut. The heat of his big body charged the air, his vitality as breathtaking as it had always been. She curled her fingers against her palm to keep from touching him.

His right hand, large, square and rawboned, twitched atop his lap and he suddenly jerked awake, sending the ledger toppling to the floor with a thud.

Black eyes clashed with hers and she flinched. Before she had time to withdraw, he was on his feet, his fingers gripping her shoulders and his expression an inscrutable blend of emotions she didn't dare label. His scent, clean and dark and masculine, catapulted her back to their shared past and weakened her knees. He smelled like the vineyard, like coiled vines and crushed grapes and sun-heated soil. He smelled like the Rafael she'd vowed never to see again.

"Sophia?" His grip tightened while everything stopped

except the flood of color that burnished his dark cheeks and brow. "Is that you?"

She didn't want his presence to strip her of her composure, her strength, or her intent to remain detached and aloof. But she wasn't surprised that it did. He'd always had the power to expose her for the yearning, desperate wretch that she was. Seeing him and feeling his powerful, unyielding touch filled her with a sharp exhilaration and a raw, terrible desire for more. Logic didn't matter. The promise of pain didn't matter. Nothing mattered but Rafael. Here. Now. "Yes," she said huskily as the sting of tears burned her eyes and the back of her nose.

"Impossible." The denial came on a shuddering breath.

Her entire body trembled between his strong hands while her vision blurred and her throat tightened. She *wasn't* immune to him, no matter what lies she told herself; she never had been. And seeing him now, so different and yet still the same, completely undid her.

His fingers rose to track the fragile ridge of her quivering jaw, tunneling beneath the hair at her nape and then tipping her head back with exquisite tenderness. Her lashes drifted closed as she felt his head dip closer. Parted lips skimmed her brow, the quivering flesh over her right eye and the sensitive swell of cheek beneath her trembling lashes. And then his grip against the back of her skull tightened and his tenderness vanished beneath an urgent demand for more. Swiftly, he reached for the curve of her buttock, the top of her thigh, and then he hauled her close against his implacable heat.

His lips descended to claim hers with hot, pressing command. He fed upon her, giving her no time to retract the invitation of her arching body.… She reached for him, molding her hands around his lean cheeks and scraping her palms over the night's growth of bristle. A low growl of pleasure, of unmet need, rumbled deep in his throat as he pulled her up to her toes and ground his hips against hers. Grateful for the support of his steely embrace, she clung to him, tasted him, burned for him.

Breaking for breath, Rafael lifted his dark head and stared down at her with dazed black eyes. "You can't be here."

"I know." Their breath mingled in the narrow space between their mouths and a shiver claimed her skin. "But after I heard—"

He cut off her explanation with a brutal, demanding kiss. His tongue probed deeply, aggressively staking his claim and challenging her to answer in kind. He again reached for her head, cupping it between his big palms as he angled her mouth for his pleasure. She gripped him above his elbows and gave everything he demanded, her fingers digging into the knotted muscles of his hard, thick arms.

Rafael groaned, his exhale guttering against her cheek as they strained together. He plowed his fingers through her hair, tangling his hands in the tawny length before tipping her throat back. Dragging his hot mouth along its curved length, she felt as if his hunger would consume her. Immolate her.

And, oh, how she wanted it.

Wanted him. Still.

His breath quickened, his pulse raced beneath her reaching hands, and she realized they both teetered on the edge of control. She didn't protest when he effortlessly boosted her up to the desk's long stretch of oiled walnut and then stepped between her spread thighs. His mouth found hers, plundering deep and sweet, feeding her with scorching, drugging kisses.

He leaned over her, the bulwark of his shoulders and

braced arms bowing her back until she struggled to remain upright. She clung to his neck as she felt his hands tug at her silk robe, yanking it from beneath her buttocks and thighs until she felt cool, polished wood against the backs of her legs. And then his hands were at her hips, delving beneath the hem of her shirt and tracking heat up her bare back and spine.

His palms rounded her ribs and his thumbs curved under the soft weight of her breasts. Her nipples immediately hardened, straining toward him through thin white cotton. His gaze slid down and his nostrils flared on a sharp inhale. Before she had a chance to divine his intent, his dark head lowered. A jolt of sensation arrowed to her core as his hot, damp mouth covered her. She jerked reflexively when his teeth clamped gently over one aching tip and a whimper slid from her throat as she squirmed upward.

Rafael lifted his head to stare at her, his eyes so dilated she couldn't discern the transition from pupil to iris. And then his hands were gripping her hips, his fingertips branding heat and intent through the thin fabric of her shorts. He hauled her to the edge of the desk, his breath coming in harsh, uneven gusts as he ground his hard length against her core. He moved his jean-clad hips, pressing every thick inch of his heat along her sensitive crease and making her shudder with need. She moaned, her head listing to the side, and opened her thighs wider.

A low sound rumbled deep in his chest and he pressed closer, setting a seductive rhythm of advance and retreat that made her feel as if she were in a dream. But at the same time, she knew he was real. *This* was real. And they should stop. "Raf." Her voice trembled. Shook as much as her hands did when she reached for his face. "Raf—"

But he was kissing her again, his tongue delving deep

while his hands and thighs moved in urgent, demanding circles. Trembling and aroused, she writhed against his commanding touch. Each heated stroke wrought a deepening of her longing, a sharpening of the pleasure that built inexorably toward a peak that remained elusively out of reach.

She squirmed against him, helpless to fight the delicious, exquisite friction while her muscles tightened and tension climbed. Her hands plucked at his shoulders, her fingers scoring the white linen stretched over his back while she felt her senses narrow, open, focus and blur all at the same time. His strong fingers slid beneath her buttocks and lifted her higher, tilting her expertly against the intoxicating pressure of the rhythm he'd set. For one shuddering moment, her vision went white and her muscles tightened in expectation. A low moan escaped her throat as she hovered on the edge, her head thrown back and her nostrils flaring as she panted for breath.

But then he was gone. Cursing through gritted teeth, he heaved himself away from her to brace trembling arms against the rough, centuries-old window casing bisecting the south wall. His head sank between his uplifted arms, and his back shook with his shuddering breaths.

CHAPTER THREE

DAZED, shaken and feeling horribly bereft, Sophia struggled to her feet. Her hands reached blindly for the ties of her robe, and she cinched them tight across her middle while an awful, yawning emptiness robbed her legs of their strength. She inched her way carefully toward Rafael, unsure of what to say. Of what to feel.

It was clear from the rigidity of his body and the taut lines of his profile that he was still painfully aroused. Her fingers itched to touch him, her arms longed to wrap around his broad torso and her heart ached to hear that he'd missed her. That he hadn't forgotten her just as she hadn't forgotten him.

His voice, rough and deep, stopped her before she drew too close. "If you know what's good for you, you'll leave. Now. Before we both do something we'll regret."

She flinched, nervousness and years of wanting what she could never have paralyzing her on the spot.

After a few torturous minutes, Rafael regained his control. He straightened, slowly, and then turned to skewer her with a caustic, cold glare. "What are you doing here?"

"I heard about Papa and—"

"Why the hell didn't you tell anybody you were coming?" he interrupted harshly.

For a second, she simply stared at him, her thoughts too jumbled to form words.

"Well?"

"You'd have told me not to bother," she blurted, suddenly feeling stripped of all her defenses. She felt raw. Exposed. And more vulnerable than she'd felt in a long, long time.

"Yes, I would have," he spat. "You're not welcome here."

Sophia couldn't stop herself from glancing at his mouth, at the swollen evidence of their mutual passion, and a fresh wave of heat curled low in her belly. "You have a strange way of showing it."

A flush darkened his cheeks and his fists clenched at his sides. "You caught me by surprise," he said harshly. "I was half-asleep and I—" His throat worked with an audible swallow. "It doesn't matter. It won't happen again."

"Agreed."

"I suggest you leave. Now."

"No." She licked her top lip and swallowed, refusing to be cowed. "I'm Papa's only child. His daughter. I have every right to be here."

His black eyes turned to cold, brittle granite. "You lost that right seven years ago."

The threat of tears burned the back of her nose, but she reminded herself that he was hurting, too. That his grief surely eclipsed hers. "I understand this is a difficult time for you." She paused, inhaling to calm her quaking nerves and to gather her resolve. She could be strong, no matter how cruel Rafael chose to be. "I understand that you're still angry with me and that you don't want me here. But whether you want it or not is immaterial. I *am* here. And I'm not leaving."

"You've had enough of London?" he sneered. "Enough of your independence and *freedom?*"

Forcing a calmness she didn't feel, Sophia kept her voice even. "Not at all. I love the life I have now. I'm only here for Papa's funeral, and then I will be out of your life forever." She cocked her jaw and braced her shoulders, holding her ground despite her wish to simply disappear. "Surely, you can cope with having me underfoot for twenty-four hours."

His nostrils flared at that, but his expression remained unyielding. "Your father wouldn't have wanted you here. You should respect his wishes."

The observation only confirmed her fears, but she'd come too far to turn back now. "Yes. Well. I've never been one to honor Papa's wishes."

His mouth hardened and he shot her a withering look. "I've noticed."

So harsh and angry, he undoubtedly didn't realize how much he reminded her of the wounded, scarred boy he'd once been. "Raf," she said softly, "I can't change the past. Nor can I change how Papa chose to react to my decision to leave."

"But you can honor his reaction."

"Not if he was wrong. I didn't betray him by leaving, no matter how he chose to interpret my actions. I simply grew up. Why is that such an unforgivable offense?"

His jaw flexed as he growled, "He deserved your loyalty."

"My loyalty?" she blurted with a baffled little laugh. "Don't you mean my life?"

"Interpret it however you wish," he said with a scowl.

"No." She shook her head. "I didn't owe Papa my life simply because he showered me with gifts whenever he happened to remember I was alive."

He stared at her in mutinous silence, his rebuttal more palpable than words.

Suddenly tired of the argument she'd never be able to win, she exhaled in defeat. "Papa didn't even know me, Raf, and you know it."

"He was your father."

"Then why didn't he act like one? I was more than an unexpected side effect of a marriage that ended before it began."

"He loved you as best he could."

"He indulged me. He spoiled me, cosseted me and bought me everything a child who'd just lost her mother could possibly want. But he didn't love me. I was an inconvenience and a bother, a distraction that he'd have preferred not to have. Why else do you think he put *you* in charge of entertaining and protecting me?"

"He didn't put me in charge."

She arched a brow. "Right. You volunteered to watch over a grieving adolescent girl because you had nothing better to do."

"You were Turino's only child. His *daughter.*"

"I was never anything beyond a pretty bauble, a possession he could show off to his friends when I wasn't away at boarding school."

"You're wrong."

"No. I'm not. He loved *you,* Raf. Not me. You were the son he always wanted, and I don't begrudge you your standing in Papa's affections. But it isn't fair that you judge me for living my own life. It isn't fair that you hate me for making choices that are different from yours."

"You hurt him. Unforgivably. And you never even tried to make amends."

"What?" she blurted. "I *did* try! It was Papa who refused my letters, my phone calls and all my requests for reconciliation!"

Rafael glared at her without speaking, the knots in his jaw flexing with his denial.

"I tried for seven *years* and he refused me every time."

"You're lying."

"Why would I lie about such a thing?"

"Because that's what women do when they want something they can't have."

Stunned by the unfounded accusation, it took several seconds before she could find the words to respond. "What could I possibly want besides closure with the father who rejected me?"

"Don't pull the innocent act with me, Sophia. You want your father's money. But it's too late. You're not getting it. You're not getting anything from him."

She gaped at him, unable to merge the boy she'd loved with the harsh, unforgiving man he'd become. "You don't believe that for a minute. I know you don't."

"Then you're a fool."

"No. I couldn't care less about the money or the land or whatever it is you men get all worked up about, and you know it. I never wanted anything from Papa except his love and acceptance. I never wanted anything from this place but *you*."

"We are not going to discuss that," he intoned with a finality that made her bristle.

Sophia felt as if she'd been slapped, and she jerked her chin up to its most defensive angle. "Of course we aren't. God forbid we talk about the real reason I left, and the role you played in it. God forbid you feel guilty for driving me away."

"I won't feel guilty for a choice you made. It was your choice to leave. Not mine." He strode to the office door and yanked it wide before gesturing for her exit. "And it's too late to change your mind."

"Did you ever tell Papa about our final conversation?" she asked, stubbornly standing her ground. "Or how you kissed me the day I left?"

"Why would I?" His low voice sounded like ground glass. "It meant nothing."

Her lungs tightened, but she didn't allow him to see how his words affected her. "Right. And it meant nothing just now, when you kissed me as if you were damned and I was your only salvation."

His nostrils flared while his black eyes sparked with flame. "I told you. You surprised me. You could have been anyone and I—"

"Stop hiding," she interrupted with an angry swipe of her hand. "Tell the truth for once in your wretched life."

"I don't hide," he said, his nostrils flaring in offense. "From anything."

She barked out a bitter laugh. "You hide from *everything,* Raf. Me. Yourself. Life. Pleasure. At least have the courage to admit it."

"You don't know what you're talking about."

"Don't I? You're miserable. Anyone who's half-observant can see it."

The sudden stiffness of his features told her the assessment had hit its mark. "I've just lost the man who saved my life, the man who gave me direction and purpose and a future. Forgive me for not being happy."

Remorse pricked at her conscience, but she wasn't going to apologize for speaking the truth. "You were miserable long before Papa's heart attack. You ignore your own desires and live your life based on what you believe *he* wanted." Conscious of his dark glare, she wondered if he'd even heard her. If he could ever hear anything she said. "That's no way to live."

"If I wanted life advice from a spoiled, selfish socialite

with no sense of family loyalty," he said in a voice full of suppressed wrath, "I would have asked."

She felt the color drain from her face. Her throat and the back of her nose burned. But she refused to let him make her cry. She'd wasted enough tears on Rafael already. "At least I know how to be happy. And how to forgive," she said before stalking past him and out into the dark hall.

Rafael had no memory of driving home, only that he somehow ended up in his big, empty master suite of black and brown. Muttering a guttural curse, he strode to his marble bathroom and cranked on the faucet. Filling both hands with icy water, he dipped his head and drenched his face with cold recriminations and arctic fury.

How could he have been so stupid?

Christ. He was paying the price for his sins, cast into a hell that had been exquisitely fashioned just for him.

How else to explain the nebulous transition between reality and dream that had stripped him of his typical control and reserve? Sophia's unexpected appearance, after seven years of absence, had caught him so off guard, he'd reacted as if she were a figment of his fevered imagination. By the time he'd come to himself, by the time he'd realized that the softness of her mouth, the small whimpering sounds within her arched throat and the curves of her breasts were *real,* it had been too late.

He'd already revealed his weakness for her, a weakness he'd sworn never to feel again. Ever. The fact that mere seconds in her presence had completely eradicated his carefully crafted control terrified him. Infuriated him. Unleashed the beast he'd kept successfully hidden for years.

So he'd lashed out at her in an effort to regain his equilibrium. He'd pushed her away with harsh words and angry accusations, refusing to show any signs of softness toward her. He needed her to hate him, to stay far, far away. He couldn't allow otherwise. She'd wounded Turino and out of loyalty to the man who'd saved him, he'd never offer her forgiveness for it. He *couldn't.*

She was better off in London, he brutally reminded himself. Despite the attraction that still flared between them, *nothing* could ever come of it.

Nothing *would* ever come of it.

In the seven years since Sophia had been gone, he'd aligned himself with Turino's efforts to cut her out of their lives. And even though he knew his mentor was overreacting, Rafael had welcomed the opportunity to eliminate Sophia from his thoughts, from his life, from his very soul. He'd convinced himself it was right to hate her, to reject her, to keep her away from her birthright. Because to do otherwise was unbearable.

If he allowed himself to think for even one minute that Turino would have wanted her home, that she belonged in California, he'd be right back where he'd been before she left.

He'd be wanting a woman he couldn't have, a woman who deserved better than Rafael Chaves. Sophia, whether her father's outcast or not, deserved better than a man possessed of a defective character, a man whose past didn't bear scrutiny.

No matter that she'd been the innocent victim of her father's stubborn resistance, he couldn't behave as if all was forgiven. He couldn't allow her to believe returning was an option. He couldn't have her close. Ever.

Seeing her again, hearing her claims, and feeling her beneath his hands and mouth had touched something deep inside, something he had to resist. He couldn't soften.

Couldn't welcome her back as if the past had never happened.

The price of doing so was too high.

She'd accused him of hiding. Of suppressing his own desires.

What she didn't understand was *why.*

His own mother had mistreated him, had sold him and his baby brother into a virtual slavery too horrific to even revisit in memory. And even though he didn't understand why the woman who'd borne him hadn't loved him, he knew on some fundamental level that she'd been right to reject him. She'd seen him for the degraded monster that he was, and the violence of his past only proved her point. If Sophia were the woman she claimed to be, she deserved better than a brute, better than a man with blood on his hands.

Rafael postponed sleep for as long as possible, retreating to his office and using his restless energy to process the last few weeks' worth of business contracts and production costs. A little after 5:00 a.m. and exhausted from nearly a week with little to no rest, he finally sank into bed and claimed a fitful sleep.

Dreams plagued him from the moment his eyes closed, torturing him with visions of Sophia in all her naked glory. Deep within his subconscious mind, he took all she offered, kissing her satiny flesh and pleasuring her as she writhed beneath him.

He consumed her as she cried into his mouth and arched beneath his questing hands, tasting her as he'd always craved. She clung to him with welcoming arms, her slim, white thighs spread wide to accommodate every yearning, seeking inch of him as he thrust deeply within her heated core. Knowing that he'd crossed a line that should never, *ever* be crossed, Rafael jerked awake to find himself twisted in his solitary sheets…frustrated, tense and uncomfortably aroused.

A frigid shower did little to bring relief, the heat of his desire for Sophia burning too close to the surface. As much as he wished otherwise, he knew he'd have to see her at Turino's funeral this morning, to pretend he hadn't kissed her, that he knew nothing of her breasts within his hands, her mouth beneath his, her soft, bare thighs cradling his. He'd have to shove aside the memory of her warmth, of the way her expression had transformed from stunned surprise to drugging desire to brittle, hurt resolve.

Simmering with banked tension, he dressed with savage motions, jerking the bleached Egyptian cotton shirt and designer silk suit over his big body. As much as he'd prefer to avoid seeing Sophia again, Turino deserved to be honored by the man he'd treated as a son. So he'd get through the funeral. He'd tolerate the hell of being near Sophia, wanting her and not touching her.

And God help him, he'd do it without betraying one atom of the turmoil beneath his skin.

CHAPTER FOUR

DESPITE Rafael's early arrival, Sophia was already in the cathedral's empty vestibule when he entered, standing with her profile to him and looking so beautiful it made his gut twist. At her side, a tall stranger with blond hair and narrow hands murmured to Dolores about their trip from London.

"Turino's passing came as such a shock," he said in the cultured tones of an English aristocrat as he turned to exchange a mournful glance with Sophia. "But as soon as we heard, we knew we needed to come to California."

We? Who was this man to Sophia?

"I'm glad you were able to accompany her," said Dolores as she leaned to place a grateful hand on the man's wrist. "Losing a father can be so difficult."

"Yes," he said as he patted Dolores's gnarled fingers and nodded solemnly. "But my Sophia is a strong woman. She'll get through it."

His Sophia?

Dolores must have sensed Rafael's arrival, because she looked over her shoulder while a soft smile split her lined face. "Raf!" she called as she bustled forward to tug at his arm. "Look who's come home!"

Scowling, Rafael resisted her efforts to draw him into the loose triangle they'd formed. His glare bounced between Sophia and the interloper as they shifted their attention to him. He hated the way the two of them matched, the way the stranger's tall, blond and blue-eyed handsomeness provided a perfect complement to Sophia's golden beauty. "Why is he here?" he asked.

"I invited him," Sophia said.

"This is hardly the time for entertaining," he said harshly.

Her blue eyes flashed with irritation. "Alexander is my friend and I want him here." The tone of her voice told him she valued the stranger's friendship far more than she valued Rafael's opinion.

"This isn't about what you want," he spat back. "It's about Turino. About honoring the dead."

"Raf!" scolded Dolores.

The stranger offered a conciliatory smile and strode forward with one long hand extended. "Alexander Bennett," he offered. "You must be the Rafael I've heard so much about."

"Funny. I haven't heard a thing about you," he said with a dismissive glance at the proffered hand.

Bennett stared at him with intelligent, mildly amused eyes and lowered his hand. "I'm not surprised. Sophia reports she hasn't conversed with you in years."

"Do you blame me?" Sophia observed, a slight note of censure coloring her tone. She moved to Bennett's side and glared haughtily at Rafael. "He doesn't exactly invite a warm, newsy exchange, does he?"

Viewing the two of them together caused Rafael's stomach to clench in protest. Though he knew she could never belong to him, the thought of her being with another man was nearly intolerable. Forcing his muscles to relax, he donned a grim smile that felt more like a baring of his teeth. "Sophia abandoned her father when he needed her most," he said, seeking refuge in harsh words and anger. "We haven't had much reason to speak since then."

"What Raf fails to mention is that—"

A large, somberly clad family crowded into the vestibule, reminding them all of the occasion that had precipitated this uncomfortable reunion.

"Dolores?" Rafael interrupted as he turned to the housekeeper. He schooled his features into the inscrutable mask of calmness he always wore and offered her his arm. "Shall we find our seats?"

Dolores, who'd watched the entire tableau with a worried expression, pursed her lips and nodded before accepting his crooked elbow. "Of course. Father Rapetti said the front left pew is reserved for us."

"Good," he said as he ushered Dolores toward the doors to the sanctuary.

"Wait," Dolores said as she turned aside to collect Sophia and Bennett. "Come," she said, beckoning them forward with one hand. "Join us."

"That's all right," Sophia hedged, her blue gaze flitting from the gathering mourners to Dolores and Rafael and then back again. "Alexander and I can just sit in—"

"Nonsense," Dolores said as she reached for Sophia's hand. "You're his daughter. You belong up front with us."

Rafael watched Dolores as she tried to convince Sophia, his chest heating with anger. "Dolores. Don't. She shouldn't be with us," he said, tipping his head toward Sophia. "She knows it as well as we do."

"Raf!" sputtered Dolores. "Sophia didn't—"

"Turino wouldn't even want her here, let alone in the front pew."

Sophia's lush mouth flattened. "You know what, Dolores? You're right." She looped her free hand through

Bennett's arm and dragged him forward. "I *am* his daughter. And I think we *will* sit up front with you. Thank you."

"No," Rafael growled. "It's an insult to even pretend—"

"Hold up there," interjected Bennett, "funerals aren't just about the person who has passed on. They're for the survivors who are left behind. They're intended to be a family's last forum for healing and forgiveness."

Rafael turned to glare at the interfering idiot, the urge to plow his fist into the pretty boy's pleasant, condescending face exploding inside him. It required supreme effort to keep his hands at his sides and away from the bastard's imperious neck. "With all due respect, *Alexander,* no one asked for your opinion."

The blond bristled, straightening to his full height and squaring off in front of Rafael. "I'll have you know, I—"

"Stop it," hissed Sophia as she moved to lift a hand to each of their chests. "Both of you. This is not the place or time to debate the issue. Let's just get through this without creating a scene. Please."

Rafael was excruciatingly aware of the press of her small, warm palm against his sternum, and he wanted to yank her away from the interloper who stared at him with flared nostrils and arched brows.

"*Nobody* has the right to talk to you that way, Sophia," Bennett reminded her, a note of pique sharpening his voice.

"You're right," she soothed as she tipped her head toward him and offered a soft smile. "But Raf is upset and grieving. We can grant him a little leeway."

Rafael did not like the patronizing tone of her voice, nor did he care for the way she rounded on him with a frown. "However, you are being impossibly rude to Alexander, for no reason other than because you're angry with me. That is not acceptable."

Scowling, he merely glared right back.

"I don't care how protective you are of Papa's wishes or how much you regret what happened last night," she snapped as she poked him in the chest with one pointed finger. "You don't attack my friends."

He stiffened while Dolores and Bennett grew suddenly alert.

"What happened last night?" Bennett asked in a low voice as he lifted a hand to Sophia's shoulder and pulled her around to face him. "Did he hurt you?"

"Of course not," she said as she tossed another caustic glance toward Rafael. "We simply had an argument about my unexpected return."

"An argument?" repeated Bennett. "Who could possibly argue with an angel like you?"

Sophia's features softened as she smiled at Bennett. "My point exactly." But a scowl reclaimed her golden brows when she returned her focus to Rafael. "Both Alexander and I will remain here until the funeral is over, whether you agree with our presence or not. And we will sit in the front pew. Deal with it. You being rude will only make things more unpleasant for all of us."

As if he cared one iota about making things pleasant for any of them.

Dolores turned to place a tentative hand upon Rafael's rigid arm. "Raf? May I speak with you for a moment in private?"

The moment they were out of hearing range, Dolores rounded on Rafael. "What on earth is wrong with you?"

Angry and aroused and frustrated with his inability to reign in his emotions, Rafael snapped, "She shouldn't be here."

"She's his *daughter,*" she scolded, reminding him of the truth with mild exasperation. "And she has a right to be here. Why are you being so difficult?"

"Turino wouldn't want her here."

"Well, Turino was a stubborn, narrow-minded fool, God rest his soul. And I can't believe you want to deny Sophia her final chance to say goodbye to the father who virtually abandoned her."

"She's the one who left," he argued mulishly.

"It doesn't matter. It happened. It can't be changed. Nothing good can come from provoking Sophia and her nice colleague. It won't make you any less angry and it certainly won't bring Turino back."

"Bennett shouldn't be here."

"Why not? He's her friend."

"I don't like the way he looks at her," he said fiercely.

"Sophia's a beautiful woman, as much as you pretend not to notice," Dolores reminded him with a cluck of her tongue. "It's only natural that she'd have an admirer or two."

Rafael scowled. "He's too old for her."

Dolores's brow furrowed with her perplexed frown. "He's no older than you."

"Exactly."

She cocked her graying head as she studied his face. "Surely, you don't begrudge her a bit of happiness and support from a man who's obviously in love with her?"

An abrupt lurch of his lungs made Rafael feel like he'd run headlong into a low-lying branch. But he breathed through it, keeping his expression unaffected and calm. "Of course I don't," he forced himself to say.

"Alexander Bennett is a good man and he's been a good friend to Sophia." She shot him a pointed glance. "Unlike you, apparently."

"I never claimed to be her friend," he muttered.

"You certainly like to act that way," she concurred with a disappointed frown. "But I know better. Why would you want to make Sophia believe her friendship never meant anything to you?"

"It didn't," he lied.

"Fine. You were never friends. But now she's back. Would it kill you to welcome her for the few hours that she is here?"

Yes.

"I'll be civil. It's the best I can offer."

Less than a week later, Rafael stood at Turino's grave with his fists knotted hard beside his thighs and his gut twisted up tight beneath his ribs. Staring at the polished marble stone and the fresh mounded earth, which was already dotted with grass and small white flowers, he grappled with emotions he didn't wish to feel. Betrayal. Hurt. Anger.

Guilt.

And fear. Fear most of all.

Sucking in a breath, he closed his eyes and relived the awful, unexpected shock of hearing Turino's will.

How could he have been so wrong about the man to whom he owed everything?

How could he have been so wrong about *her?*

Rafael thought he'd known Dante Turino better than any person on Earth. He thought he'd understood the big, gruff man's cold rejection of his only daughter. Rafael had known Turino's resistance to change, the finality of his decisions, his capacity to carry a grudge. He'd lived with the man's bullish personality, his stubborn commitment to a path once he'd stepped upon it, for close to two decades. There was no negotiating with Turino. Ever. He never admitted his mistakes. Never revisited a decision once it had been made.

So why now?

Why had he done it?

Rafael remembered his mentor as he'd last seen him. Turino, silent and pale within his network of tubes and needles, had been reduced to a weak invalid who was nothing like the big American who'd saved Rafael's life so many years before. Having their roles reversed and watching his mentor struggle for breath had made Rafael feel off-kilter, disoriented and infuriatingly incapable of making things right again.

"Turino?" he'd whispered as he'd leaned to touch the man's rawboned shoulder.

Turino had shifted on his adjustable bed and slowly dragged his eyes open. "Raf," he'd said through cracked lips. "You're here."

"Where else would I be?" Rafael had forced an encouraging smile. "Dolores said you were asking for me."

Turino's eyelids had slid closed again while his hand groped blindly for Rafael's wrist.

Rafael had moved to accommodate him, pressing his palm over the back of Turino's hand and bending low over his cracked, moving lips. "What is it?" he'd asked.

"Promise me…" Turino's voice drifted to silence while he struggled for breath.

"Anything."

Distress had pulled at the corners of Turino's mouth and his closed eyelids had trembled as he'd soundlessly repeated the words.

"I promise," Rafael had urged, his heart contracting with worry. "Just tell me."

"Good boy… So glad…" He'd hauled in a shallow breath and his grip had tightened like talons upon Rafael's arm. "Dying. I need to…"

A prickling sense of fear had rippled beneath the surface of Rafael's skin. "You're not dying."

"Yes…" Turino's low voice had been terrifyingly earnest. A rattle of breath, too thin to possibly keep anyone alive for long, had fueled his next words with feeble, thready strength. "Too late. I want…"

"It's not too late." Panic had built within Rafael's chest, making his ribs feel too small to contain the rising alarm as Turino's head lolled listlessly to the side. Rafael had shaken Turino's shoulder, his voice sharp. "You can fight this, damn it. Stay with me."

His demand had been met with the horrible, inescapable whine of a machine, its single, high-pitched tone proclaiming Turino's exit from the world with more finality than a death knell. For several long seconds, Turino's hand had retained its grip upon Rafael's wrist, until, all at once, it had relaxed and fallen to the white mattress.

"Nurse!" Rafael had screamed, a keening denial crowding close on the heels of his call for help.

In the frenzy of activity and funeral preparations that had followed, Raf had spent little time trying to make sense of Turino's disjointed last words. It wasn't until the reading of Turino's will that everything had clicked into place. *Promise me.*

And he'd promised.

Never knowing what he'd promised to do, he'd promised.

Plowing his hand through his hair, Rafael stared down at the damp ground and swallowed back the lump of guilt clotting his throat.

He couldn't do it.

No matter that Turino had wanted it, no matter that the stubborn man had finally forgiven Sophia her betrayal. No matter the promise he'd made to the only man who'd ever given a damn about him. He couldn't.

Just thinking of it, Rafael was catapulted back to the day he'd awoken on Turino lands, to the day his harsh life of pain and degradation had been replaced by one of purpose and acceptance.

Before that day, hunger and fear had been Rafael and his little brother Paolo's constant companions. Raised in one *casabre* after another, trying to sleep in grimy closets while the muffled grunts of *Mamãe* and her clients kept them awake, eating food they scavenged from restaurant garbage, and never, ever complaining when a customer kicked at them with his pointed boots, Paolo and Rafael had learned to survive without any expectation of softness or kindness. They learned to act like the *ratos de esgoto* they were, to lie, fight and steal from the privileged and wealthy who occasionally deigned to skirt the edges of their decaying neighborhood.

They'd have continued to adulthood on the same path had their mother not sold them to *o homem rico* with yellow hair, cold hands and even colder eyes. *Mamãe* had promised that things would be better, that the rich man would feed them and dress them in fine clothes.

Like so many other times in her depraved life, *Mamãe* had been wrong.

Rafael had thought he'd known fear before, but when his new owner tied them down and then proceeded to brand them with his mark of ownership, the stench of burning flesh and the sound of his brother's screams were forever imprinted in his mind.

A year later, after finding little Paolo's lifeless body broken and abused, Rafael had known a rage so fierce it had turned his soul black. He had no goodness inside him anymore. It had died the day he'd failed to save his brother. And he'd become a monster, blind to conscience, when he'd attacked the man who'd sacrificed both their souls.

It wasn't until the monster had fallen, his head hitting the marble floor with a sickening crack, that Rafael realized what he'd done. Panicked, he'd run. He'd run until his lungs burned and his bare feet were cut and bleeding. He didn't remember falling, didn't remember much of anything until he awoke several days later in a richly appointed room he didn't recognize.

He'd never lain in a bed before, never felt anything softer than hard concrete beneath his back. He'd tried to rise, but failed, the edges of his vision turning black as pain assailed him. Collapsing back against the white mattress, he hissed a furious, impotent breath through his teeth.

"Lie still," a strange man with a gruff voice said, pressing a wide, cool hand against his shoulder. "You'll rip open your stitches."

Much later, Rafael learned the large man—he called himself Turino—had found him collapsed at the side of the road, unconscious and covered in his own blood. The stranger was tall and broad, and possessed a manner so suspiciously pragmatic that Rafael stiffened defensively whenever he came in the room. He didn't trust the stranger's big hands, the medicines he tried to coax him to take. He wanted nothing from the man who insisted on saving him. He didn't want to be saved. He didn't deserve to live, and so he refused every overture the man made, trading snarling hostility and fury for bandages and broths and medicine.

Rafael spoke only one time, when the man had asked about the brand upon his right flank, the overlapping letters of ridged flesh spelling out *escrivo* in Portuguese.

"Who did this to you?"

"A demon," he'd answered through clenched teeth. "When he made me one of his minions."

"Of course," the man had said in a calm voice. "I believe I might have a cure for that."

Stupid *tolo,* Rafael had thought. As if there were any cure besides death for one with a soul as dark as his.

As soon as he could move without losing consciousness, he started making plans to leave. There was nothing for him here, no reason to stay in the home of this random stranger who'd saved him. And despite the kindness Turino had shown him, Rafael knew he didn't deserve softness or safety. Not after the way he'd failed to protect Paolo.

The day after his fever had broken, Rafael waited until Turino had headed out to the fields and the fat housekeeper had departed for her daily trip to the market, before he slowly sat up. The pain of movement made him wince, but he dressed in the cleaned and mended clothing that had been left for him on the nightstand beside a glass of water. The worn denims and thin, gray shirt smelled like this place, like sun and earth and safety and acceptance.

He hated it.

But the clothes were his only possessions, the only things he could claim as his own.

He moved with painstaking slowness, his healing body protesting every arduous motion. Ignoring the pounding headache that tightened his scalp and the stabbing pain in his feet, he forced himself to continue his preparations to leave. He shoved the containers of medicine into the white pillowcase he'd taken from the bed, rationalizing that Turino would have no need of them after he was gone. He hated that he needed the crutch of drugs, but he wasn't foolish enough to believe he could finish healing without them.

After the eternity it took for him to dress, he took a moment to rest, grappling with the dual desires to escape and simply give up the fight altogether. Cocking his head, he listened for sounds of movement, a small, unacknowledged part of himself hoping for interference.

None came.

When he was sure no one was around to stop him, he placed his battered feet on the floor and forced himself to stand. Spikes of pain arrowed up his legs and blackness claimed the edges of his vision. Gasping, he sank back down to the mattress, gripping its edge while his head sank low between his bowed shoulders.

Cristo, he hurt.

"What are you doing?" a small voice asked from the opened doorway.

He turned to face the door with a snarl, unprepared for both the question and the company. "Go away."

Turino's pretty little princess of a daughter didn't even flinch, her expression both innocent and curious.

The stupid girl didn't realize the danger she was in, her big, blue eyes unworried and unafraid. She'd visited him every day, peering around the edge of the door whenever he'd been left alone. No matter how he'd scowled at her and barked at her to leave him alone, she'd never once shown fear. Each time she grew bolder, inching a bit closer and talking soothing nonsense to him as if he were some stray dog she meant to tame. Compared to her angel face, white skin and golden hair, he'd felt like a wild animal. And knowing the comparison was accurate, he made a point of snarling and snapping at her, his only motive to scare her away.

He didn't like the way the girl made him feel. The scent and sound of her, soft and sweet and finer than anything he'd ever known, made his heart pound. Her nearness made it hard to breathe.

"Why are you dressed?" she persisted in a sensible tone as she inched toward him. "You'll get blood all over your clothes again."

"None of your business," he growled. "Get out of here before the *papão* gets you."

Emboldened, she shook her head and moved ever closer. "You're not leaving, are you?"

"What's it to you?"

Twin lines appeared between her golden brows. "But you can't leave. You're hurt."

"I'm fine."

She leaned to press her pale hand to his forehead, the cool touch of her fingers making his insides seize up in response.

Before he was even aware that he'd moved, he'd gripped her wrist and yanked her hand away with a grunt.

Her eyes widened, but she didn't try to pull free. Instead, she merely relaxed within his grip and stared at him with a calm, curious expression. "You don't have to go, you know," she told him. "Papa said you could live here for as long as you wanted."

Rafael knew he should release her, knew that touching her was wrong. She was delicate. Innocent. Too weak to withstand the devastation that knowing him would bring. But he couldn't bring himself to let her go. Not yet.

"He said a bad man hurt you."

He killed my brother.

Her small pink mouth pursed in offense as her gaze tracked his bruised and battered face. "I hope you hurt him back."

I did.

"What's your name?" she asked, cocking her head as she lifted her eyes back to his.

He knew he should remain silent, that he should send her away. But the urge to keep her with him, to draw out the sweetness of her company, overwhelmed his better judgment. "Rafael."

She smiled, and it was as if the sun had broken through a dark, angry cloud. "Nice to meet you, Raf. I'm Sophia."

Inwardly alarmed at the way her smile made his throat thicken, he dropped his eyes to his hand upon her tender flesh. Wincing at the tight half-moons of white his dark fingertips pressed into her skin, he forced his grip to loosen and shoved her arm away. "You shouldn't be here," he told her. "Turino told you to stay out of this room."

"Papa thinks I'm a baby," she confided with a haughty huff of breath. "But I'm not. I'm practically grown. And I know you won't hurt me."

You're wrong.

"Where do you go to school?" she asked, the shift in conversational topic setting him off-kilter.

Mortified, he felt his face heat. He'd watched other boys come and go from school, dressed in their clean uniforms of navy and white. He'd hated those spoiled, pampered boys with their overprotective mothers and polished shoes. He'd hated them with a hot fierceness, with a violence that led him to throw rocks at the backs of their skinny, white legs. "I don't go to school."

Her brows arched into perfect crescents of gold. "You don't go to school?" she repeated. "But who teaches you?"

Rafael swallowed back his embarrassment, suddenly angry at this stupid, silly girl who knew so little of the real world. "Nobody," he mumbled sullenly.

Her narrow hand lifted to his hot cheek. "I'll teach you, then. We'll have school every day until you're well."

Her offer surprised him. It made his chest tighten and his eyes smart. Bewildered and disturbed, he swallowed back the bite of hope her words wrought. He wasn't worth her time. He wasn't worth teaching. He didn't belong in her world, in the world of civilized, educated men.

She hadn't seemed to notice.

Nor, he found to his consternation, had Turino. Through some unspoken, tacit agreement, it was decided that playing teacher to the wounded stray was the perfect summer diversion for Sophia. And so Rafael found himself her reluctant pupil, subjected to her organized schedule of reading, math and history lessons.

By the time summer ended, they'd worked their way through her entire supply of textbooks. He spent his mornings in the fields, earning his keep among the vineyard workers, and his afternoons in the study with Sophia. And when she left again for London, he devoted his days and nights to repaying his debt to Turino, to mastering everything he could learn about the wine-making business.

And so their years had progressed. Until Sophia's mother had died and Sophia had come to California to stay.

Until she'd become a woman and everything had changed.

Until she'd left for London a final time and his world had turned bleak and dark once again. He'd only survived it by seeking refuge in anger and hard work, by joining Turino in his rejection of the woman they'd both loved.

Shaking himself out of his reverie, Rafael stared blindly at Turino's headstone. He didn't know how to navigate his world now, didn't know how to bring Sophia back without jeopardizing everything. Keeping her in London was safer, but it would keep him from honoring his promise. It would keep him from honoring Turino.

But if he brought her back…

Oh, God, if he brought her back…

His chest tightened painfully, while his ribs and lungs and throat knotted with trepidation. He wasn't strong enough to go back to the way it had been before.

From the very first time he'd seen her, he'd been lost. She'd never been frightened of him, despite his bruises, his fierce scowls, his unkempt hair and big, brutal body. With her wide blue eyes, angelic features and golden hair, she'd been the first beautiful thing in his pathetic life. She hadn't been afraid. She'd accepted him. Teased him. Laughed with him.

He sucked in a thready inhale, his hands trembling against his thighs.

She'd loved him. And he wasn't strong enough to refuse her a second time.

He might have been. Once. He might have even convinced himself that Sophia didn't matter, that he could relegate his earlier obsession with her to the annals of his past. She was just a woman, he'd reasoned, just one of a million beautiful faces who populated the world. Once, he might have thought he could keep her at arm's length. Ignore her and feel nothing.

He was wrong.

Now, after tasting her, touching her, dreaming of her again, he knew he'd overestimated his immunity to her. He couldn't go back.

No matter what Turino mandated from the grave.

CHAPTER FIVE

"MS. TURINO?" Trudy's urgent whisper accompanied the soft scrape of the boardroom door against the plush maroon-and-cream carpet.

Stifling her expression of surprise, Sophia smiled at her gathered clients, offered a quick apology for the interruption and then exited her chair to join the firm's receptionist at the threshold. The fastidious matron looked atypically pink and flustered, enough to cause Sophia concern. "What is it?" she asked.

Trudy's fingers fluttered over her sternum while she visibly tried to calm herself.

Worried, Sophia placed a hand on Trudy's rounded shoulder. "Are you all right?" she asked, her voice pitched low. "Is something wrong?"

"No." Trudy dropped her gaze while her breath remained rapid and shallow. "It's just that…someone is here to see you." Her faint, thready whisper was barely audible and her flushed cheeks betrayed an agitation Sophia had never seen before. "A man who claims to knows you."

Confused by the fact that the staid woman was behaving completely out of character, she asked, "You interrupted my meeting because a prospective client claims to have met me before?"

"No. Yes. Oh, it's not the same," Trudy stammered in

a flustered whisper. "He's different." She cast a furtive glance at Sophia's gathered clients and whispered, "He's… quite compelling."

Sophia arched one brow and straightened, surprised to realize that the practical, no-nonsense receptionist had noticed *anything* beyond the man's business needs. "Then schedule an appointment with him."

Trudy shook her head. "It's urgent. He needs to speak with you immediately."

Sophia held on to her patience with effort, reassuring her clients with a swift smile. "I'm sure he does. But we're addressing urgent issues in here as well. Please inform him that I'll be available at noon."

Trudy licked her lips and blushed anew, her hands twisting at her waist. "He'll be upset that I didn't fetch you."

Incredulous, Sophia stared at the receptionist. Trudy was known for her stoic adherence to protocol, and she was *always* immune to the efforts of cocky, flirtatious clients intent on bending the rules. The fact that this stranger had managed to turn Trudy into a nervous bird of fluttering agitation both amazed and intrigued Sophia. "Then blame the delay on me. Tell the gentleman that we value each of my clients equally and that he will simply have to wait until I am free. As he's a businessman himself, I'm sure he will appreciate the sentiment."

The tidy brunette's face settled into a pained grimace and she cleared her throat noisily as she shifted from one sensible heel to the other. "Yes, Ms. Turino. I apologize. It's just that—"

"Now."

Trudy's mouth pursed into a distressed knot, but she bobbed her head once and backed out of the room.

When the door clicked closed, Sophia returned to her clients and offered a blinding smile. "Now where were we?"

Forty minutes later, she concluded her meeting with a lucrative agreement that would benefit all involved, dismissed her clients and gathered the marketing materials they'd selected. "Trudy," she called as she exited the boardroom. "I'm in the mood for sushi. Would you call in an order for me?"

"Trudy's gone. I sent her out for an early lunch."

"You sent—?" The familiar masculine voice registered a beat too late, sending a ripple of recognition down Sophia's spine. Disbelieving, she turned to find Rafael standing in the center of the firm's posh cream-and-burgundy waiting area. He held a thick manila envelope in his right hand and wore an expression more intense than any she'd seen. "Raf," she breathed, her muscles suddenly weak. "What are you doing here?"

He seemed to fill the entire space with his formidable presence. "You left before the reading of your father's will."

Sophia gaped at him in silence, stunned that he'd come all this way to reiterate something she already knew.

"You should have been there," he said, his dark, foreboding expression reminding her of all the things she'd left behind. Of all the things she didn't wish to remember.

A disbelieving laugh knotted in her chest. "As you so ruthlessly pointed out," she said, recovering her voice even though her pulse refused to settle. "Papa no longer thought of me as his daughter, nor did he wish for me to return for his funeral. Why on earth would I remain to hear a will that excluded me?"

A flash of irritation darkened his black eyes. "Because it didn't."

"What?"

"Your father left you everything. The land, his half of the winery, the estate, all of it."

"All of..." Shock flooded her legs, making her limbs feel numb and somehow separate from her senses. She felt herself swaying, the floor tilting dangerously as the edges of her vision darkened.

He caught her before she crumpled to the floor, his big, square hand steadying her balance while her thoughts continued to spin.

She slapped his hand aside, backing away from him until her spine bumped up against Trudy's cream receptionist counter. "You're wrong," she insisted as she reached to grip its rounded edge. "Papa would have never—"

He scowled, obviously agreeing with her pronouncement. "Yet he did."

"But that would mean," she said faintly, "he wanted me to..." Her voice trailed off while options she'd never, ever considered circled wildly.

"Yes."

She shook her head, too stunned to think clearly. "But he hated me."

"He wanted you to come home. To take your place as his heir and as head of the Turino winery."

"Me? Head of the winery?" she gasped, taking a sideways step away from him. "No. This has to be some sort of cruel joke." A bubble of hysterical laughter crowded the back of her throat. "Or a clerical error of some kind."

His stony glare defied her claim. "I assure you. It's not."

"You're wrong," she insisted desperately. "You have to be."

"Turino—"

"No—" She held up a hand to ward off further explanation "—Papa just never got around to making a new will after I left. You know how he was. He lived as if he'd never die." She fluttered her fingers toward Rafael, toward the perfect surrogate son who'd never disappointed the estimable Dante Turino. "Had he taken the time to do so, he'd have named you as sole beneficiary. I'm sure of it. *You're* supposed to have everything. Not me. Not after the way he cut me off."

A dark and dangerous flash of fury, so fleeting she almost didn't catch it, flared deep within his black eyes. "Turino did rewrite his will. Twice. Once after you left for London and then once again, two days after his heart attack."

Sophia's chest tightened, making it hard to draw breath, the implications of his words cutting through the beliefs she'd always held regarding her father. The rejection she'd lived with for years. "Two days after his… But that can't be. You must be mistaken." Her grip upon the counter tightened while a tremor gained ground within her stomach. "After seven years of *nothing*—no contact, no word, no breath of forgiveness—there's no way Papa would leave everything to me. It doesn't make any sense."

He extended the manila envelope, his face an inscrutable mask of coldness. "I have the paperwork here, if you don't believe me."

She refused to even look it, at the evidence of her father's untenable whimsy, and shook her head. "No. I don't want it. It's too late. I don't want anything from him."

"What you want is irrelevant."

"No. It's *not,*" she blurted. "Don't you *dare* say that. Not now." She felt her anger build, and it lent strength to her trembling legs. "What I wanted was a *father.* Someone who loved me and knew me and allowed me to make my own choices. Not this—" she jabbed a pointed finger toward the envelope "—this token inheritance after he's already gone. I wanted a father who accepted the fact that I'd grown up, a father who respected me and wanted a relationship with me." She blinked, appalled that a sting of tears was making her vision blur. "I never wanted his land or his money or his *things.* I wanted *him.*"

"Too bad, Princess. Because this is what you've got."

She flung a hand up between them. "No. You've dedicated your life to him—it should be yours. You're his *partner,* for God's sake. So take it already. Take it and leave me to live my life."

A muscle flexed in his jaw and his black gaze bored into hers. "No."

"No?"

"Turino wanted you to have it."

Lifting her chin, she growled, "Well, Papa doesn't always get what he wants, does he?"

"He does if I have any say about it."

"Right," she concurred with an impatient huff. "I almost forgot. You live to serve my father, the perfect Saint Turino who can do no wrong. You'll follow his will no matter whose life it disrupts, whether you agree with it or not."

"Yes," he admitted while black fire flickered deep within his eyes. "I made him a promise and I intend to keep it."

"You can't promise him that *I* will do his bidding. It doesn't work that way."

"You're his daughter. The least you can do is honor his final wish, now that he's gone."

"Don't you dare lecture me, Raf. I *always* wanted to honor Papa's wishes and to be the daughter I could never be. I tried for years to make him see me. To know me. But he never did. I refuse to feel guilty for that anymore."

"Your guilt is not my problem. Nor is your allegiance. Because *mine* is to Turino, and I intend to see his will carried out."

"You can't force me to return home if I don't wish to go."

Torn between his conflicting desires to draw her close and to force her far, far away, Rafael stared at the defiant tilt of her small face and debated his next words. For Turino's sake, he had to convince her to come home. But he knew he'd never survive her proximity unless she hated him. She had to hate him. It was the only way to keep her safe from his destructive influence. So he stepped closer, and the air between them crackled with tension. "Try me," he threatened.

"You can't be serious," she blurted as she arched away from his looming presence. "I'm not a teenager, all doe-eyed and in love with you anymore. I won't jump to do your bidding just because you happen to crook your finger in my direction."

He didn't flicker so much as an eyelash, though his body clamored to convince her with hands and mouth and tongue. "You'll do as I say or else suffer the consequences."

"What consequences?" she scoffed. "You can't touch me here."

"Can't I?" He arched a brow. "I wonder how long this company will retain your services if you refuse to service my account."

"But you don't even have an account!"

"Not yet, I don't. But I'll have one within the hour if you don't agree to come home."

"Fine. Engage their marketing services," she said as the color rose in her cheeks. "My boss will most likely insist on handling your account himself."

"Not if I tell him that having you as my liaison is a condition of me signing with him."

She sent him a haughty glare. "Fine. I'll be your *liaison.* I'll sell Turino wines all over the world if I have to. But I'm not going to California with you."

"You'd rather be fired?"

"I'd rather another position."

"I'll make the same offer, no matter where you go."

"You can't do that!"

He offered her a cold, triumphant smile. "I wonder how long you'll survive here without a job."

"Longer than you'd expect," she challenged. "I just inherited my father's entire estate, remember? I have enough money that I'll never need to work again. I'll be fine, no matter what threats you make. And I'm *not* going back to California."

She'd always been a fighter, but he could tell that her years away from home had made her stronger. More resourceful. A grudging respect he didn't wish to feel warmed his gut. "Your inheritance is not liquid," he said. "It's tied up in land and the business and the estate. Once you run through your savings, you'll have nowhere else to go."

She narrowed her eyes as she stared up at him, as resistant to his bullying as she'd always been. "Then I'll sell. Everything. You've done such a fine job building the reputation of the Turino Winery, I'm sure investors will line up to pay me a premium price."

"You can't sell," he bluffed.

"Of course I can. It's mine, as you so clearly pointed out. I can do whatever I want with it now."

"Except dissolve or alter the partnership. You can't do that unless I agree." He loomed over her, and her dizzying scent rose up between them. "I don't."

"But I have a life now," she protested. "I have friends. A career I excel at. I won't give it all up for a man who didn't even acknowledge my existence for the past seven years."

"You don't have a choice. You're a Turino. The only one left."

"So?"

"So your inheritance represents the labor of eight generations of Turinos. A family legacy nearly two centuries in the making. You can't be foolish enough to throw that all away just because of some minor spat with your father."

"It wasn't a minor spat!" she shouted in frustration. "I've lived without any family contact for years because Papa was too stubborn to admit he was wrong!"

"Yes. But he wanted to make amends in the end. He forgave you."

"I did nothing that needed forgiving," she argued. "He was the one in the wrong."

"Now who's being stubborn?" he asked.

"Like you're one to talk," she shot back.

"Me?" He reared back, unwilling to discuss anything beyond Turino and her role as his heir. "This has nothing to do with me."

"It has everything to do with you." She glared at him, her color high and her breasts lifting with her agitated breaths. "By putting *you* in charge of my welfare and giving you control over my life, Papa was exacting his revenge the only way he knew how. This has nothing to do with making amends. It's just another way for him to control me, to force me into a box of his making. Except now, he's making *you* his henchman."

"Fine. I'm his henchman." He forced a grim smile. "Hate me, call me names, do whatever makes you feel better. But know that the outcome of this little meeting of ours won't change."

"Because you'll blackmail me into doing Papa's bidding."

"Your father only ever wanted what's best for you."

"No. Papa only wanted what *he* thought was best. He couldn't have cared less about what *I* thought was best."

"It's unfortunate that you choose to see it that way."

"Choose?" she sputtered incredulously. "You dare to talk to me about *choice?*"

"Yes. You could choose to view this as an opportunity, a chance to prove to your father how capable and independent you really are. You could choose to see that your father was a proud man who loved you the best he knew how, a man who offered an olive branch of peace before he died."

"Sending you to coerce me into a life I don't want is not a peace offering."

"He didn't send me. I came of my own volition."

"Liar," she countered. "You're only here because my father's will forced your hand."

"I came because it's the right thing to do," he growled, irritated that she was right. "I came because I keep my word."

"And you resent it. Just like you resented all the time you had to waste on me before," she said.

"I never resented you."

She met his claim with a bitter laugh, and knowing he was the reason for her bitterness made his stomach twist. "I know you always felt saddled with Turino's spoiled, self-absorbed, immature daughter, just as I know you felt too indebted ever to complain."

"Of course I wouldn't complain. I owe Turino everything. Watching out for you was the least I could do."

"Right. So you kept me out from underfoot," she snapped. "You *protected* me from my own impulsiveness, and you kept me *safe* from whatever dangers you and Papa imagined lurked on the horizon. But you didn't want to do any of those things. Ever. You hated the imposition and you were more than happy to see me permanently gone. Don't bother trying to deny it."

I was never happy with you gone. Ever.

"And now, thanks to Papa's *peace offering,* you're left to deal with the mess that is Sophia yet again. A mess you want even less than I do. Admit it. If you'd had any say in the matter, we wouldn't even be talking now."

Frustrated, wanting her, and unable to do anything about either, he rattled the papers between them. "I do have a say. And I'm in agreement with your father. He wanted you home, running the Turino Winery, and fulfilling your potential as his only heir. I'm sorry if you don't like it, but that's the way it is."

"Oh, I believe you're sorry," she shot back. "But you're sorry for all the wrong reasons. You're sorry, and you're taking out your frustrations on me instead of the man who deserves it."

"I'm not taking anything out on you."

"Of course you are! He's manipulating both of us, and you're playing right into his hands! He's punishing me for leaving him and he's leveraging your loyalty to exact the punishment on his behalf, knowing full well that you're too honorable to refute him. We're both just pawns in his game, and you're allowing him to continue his role of puppeteer."

"I'm not."

"You are. You hate me," she insisted while her blue eyes flashed with frustration. "You'd like nothing better than to see me cut out of everything."

What I'd like is you in my bed. Beneath me. Writhing with pleasure and screaming my name.

"So why can't you just pretend Papa wanted that, too, and end this? Now, before everything gets worse?"

"What I want is irrelevant," he boomed. "What does matter is your birthright and a dying man's last wishes."

"Why?"

"Why?"

"Yes. Why do Papa's wishes take precedence over yours?"

He didn't answer her. He couldn't. His secrets were too deeply buried, his past too horrific for her to hear.

"Why does the mere act of saving your life put you in his debt forever?"

When he met her question with more silence, she sighed and her expression softened. Dangerously. He tensed as she moved to place a tentative hand upon his rigid forearm. "You don't have to live this way, you know. You can build the life *you* want instead of the one he's prescribed for you."

He didn't want her sympathy. He didn't want her sweetness or her acceptance or her understanding. He wanted her to despise him. He *needed* her to hate him. "You don't know what you're talking about," he snarled, jerking his arm from the fire of her touch. "And I don't have time to clarify things for you. All you need to know is that I will not allow you to stand in the way of my promise to him."

"*You* won't allow me."

"Yes. We either do this the easy way, or we do it the hard way. Your choice."

"No," she repeated calmly as she stood her ground.

"No?" He glared at her, irritated that he'd yet again failed to intimidate her into doing his bidding. Just like when she was a child, his resistance, his anger and his commands only served to strengthen her resolve. She'd always possessed the ability to chip beneath his defenses, to draw him closer until he grew soft and weak and malleable. But this time, he couldn't let her win. It would ruin them both. "I don't think you understand," he reiterated. "You choose. Or I choose for you."

"You can't," she insisted with a determined jut of her

chin. "Papa might control you, but he'll never control me. Ever. His bullying tactics didn't work seven years ago, and they certainly won't work now, even if you're the one doing the bullying."

They stood in their silent standoff, until Rafael realized he'd been approaching things all wrong. How could he have forgotten? Sophia couldn't be bullied. She had to be dared. Or coaxed. But coaxing was too dangerous. For both of them. "I'm not bullying you," he said. "You're just afraid, and you're allowing fear to stand in the way of a lucrative partnership."

"Fear?" she repeated, bristling. "I'm not afraid."

"You are," he goaded, hoping that she'd rise to the bait. "The Sophia I remembered would have never backed down from a challenge. She'd have welcomed the adventure, the risk and the unknown. She'd have plunged in headfirst without a second thought, and she certainly wouldn't have kept saying no because she was afraid."

"I told you, I'm not afraid. I haven't been afraid for years."

He waved a dismissive hand toward the elegant surroundings of the firm's reception area. "You're lying. Fear is the only thing that would have allowed you to accept a life that's such a predictable, boring grind."

She stiffened, her mouth settling into an annoyed line. "Insulting me and my chosen career won't help you make your case."

He angled a contemptuous glance at the stack of plans on the receptionist's tidy desk. "It should. Your talents are wasted on accounts like—" he tipped his head to read the top file "—O'Toole Refrigeration."

"They're a perfectly respectable business," she protested.

His arched brow belied her claim. "You know you're meant for better things."

"Flattery won't help you, either," she snapped.

"It's not flattery. It's the truth."

"No," she corrected. "It's you trying to get what you want. And it won't work."

"You have no idea what I want," he said, shifting tactics yet again. As dangerous as it was, he knew he had to soften her into changing her mind. When bullying and daring failed, coaxing was the only option left.

Just think of her as a client. A beautiful, stubborn client who has to be seduced into changing her mind.

Though flirting with her as if she were a stranger and touching her as if it meant nothing was a gamble he shouldn't take, he couldn't give up until she agreed to come home. So he forced his rigid muscles to relax and his features to calm. Stepping into her space, he lifted his hand to the counter's edge, a hairbreadth from the pale, white skin of her upper arm. "I know you miss California," he said in a low, beguiling tone. "I know you miss the warmth of Napa Valley, the sun and the sense of family and home."

Visibly suspicious of his changed demeanor, she narrowed her eyes and crossed her arms. "If I miss anything, which I don't, it would be the fantasy of home. Not the reality."

"There's nothing to stop you from creating the fantasy now," he murmured as he stepped closer. Everything within him tightened, heated. But he didn't allow his expression to change. "It's yours. You can make the home you've always dreamed of having."

"That dream is dead," she said as she edged sideways, creating space between them.

"It doesn't have to be," he said. He moved until he'd trapped her between his uplifted arms, stalling her retreat.

"Working the land, crafting quality wines, it's in your blood." He leaned closer until she had to tip her head to retain eye contact. "Don't you remember how much you loved learning about the different species of grapes? The fermentation? The soil? You never ran out of questions and you always wanted to know more."

"I was a child, fruitlessly trying to impress you." Despite her defensive posture, he could hear the shallowness of her breath.

He could see the frantic flutter of her pulse at her throat, and he felt his own heartbeat slug hard and fast within his chest. "Don't you want to impress me now?" he asked quietly.

She swallowed audibly and color flagged the crests of her cheeks. "Fortunately, I've matured beyond such pointless quests."

Dragging his eyes from the evidence of her reaction, he forced a reasonable tone. "Of course you have. Which means you'll no longer allow my presence to stand in your way. You can claim your birthright without the messiness of our past interfering."

"You're right. I could. If I wanted to," she reiterated. The thinness of her voice betrayed her awareness of him. "But I don't."

"No?" He allowed his gaze to slip down to her mouth, a mouth that had parted with nervous, reluctant arousal. "But you and I both know how hard it was for you to leave California."

Her color deepened and her attention darted to his chin. "London is my home now."

"You don't love London the way you loved the winery."

Her hands clenched at her thighs while her nostrils flared. "Like I said, I loved the fantasy. I thought I loved you. I'm no longer the fool I once was."

Good. Keep it that way. "Which is why it can work now," he said evenly. "It's been seven years. You're a mature adult now."

She remained rigid and silent, her thoughts as transparent as glass as her resolve wavered.

"Come home, Soph," he cajoled, watching her translucent skin and her expressive features as she battled to resist him. "Embrace the life you were meant to have, the life your father wanted you to have."

Furrows of worry and doubt drew lines between her brows. "No."

"As full partner in the winery, you'll have more creative leeway than you'd ever have here. You can build Turino Winery into a multinational company, and market it in a way that far surpasses anything your father ever dreamed of," he promised. "Think of the freedom. The lack of boundaries."

"No."

"You won't even have to see me if you don't wish it," he added, knowing his presence contributed to her opposition. "Our interactions will be based on business only. We can even communicate through a third party if it'll make you more comfortable."

The offer to maintain the distance between them seemed to have the opposite effect from what he'd intended, as a flare of anger lit within her eyes. "You'd like that, wouldn't you?" she accused as she shoved against his chest with both hands. "Fulfilling Papa's wishes without having to get personally involved."

"It never occurred to me that you'd want it otherwise," he said as he granted her the space she demanded. A flicker of unease traveled the length of his spine, warning him to tread lightly.

"Of course it didn't," she said. "You've always been

very good at projecting your preferences and rules and boundaries onto me." Her eyes, as blue and unfathomable as the ocean, dared him to deny the claim. "Except now, you'll find I'm not the biddable little Sophia I used to be."

"You were never biddable," he reminded her as his trepidation mounted. He'd wanted her to come home, to hate him and to fit into the safe, predictable role he'd crafted for her.

"Well, I'm even less biddable now." She seemed to gain inches as she warmed to the topic. "And when I come home, *if* I come home, it won't be on your terms. It'll be on *mine*."

"Yours?"

"Yes. Mine. For once, *I'll* be the one calling the shots instead of some arrogant, unreasonable male with a penchant for secrets."

"Fine. Tell me what will convince you to come home, and I'll make it happen," he said.

CHAPTER SIX

SOPHIA stared at Rafael, trying to make sense of her conflicting emotions and faltering resolve. He really hadn't changed, despite the years of separation that yawned between them. Adaptable, angry, controlling and charming when the situation required it, he was a chameleon who adjusted his tactics until he met with success. And she, susceptible to every shade of Rafael he cared to display, was tempted to fall in line just as she always had. But she couldn't. She'd learned from her mistakes. Hadn't she? "You don't mean that," she said.

"I do."

She narrowed her eyes as she stared at him, mentally weighing the pros and cons. It was easy to believe she'd be strong enough when a physical distance stretched so irrevocably between them. She could ignore him, discount him and pretend his opinion of her didn't matter. But maintaining her professional resolve when he was close enough to touch, to smell, would be another challenge entirely. One she wasn't entirely convinced she could handle.

On the other hand, the thought of being near Rafael again, of debating various aspects of their shared business while tension kindled between them, made her feel more alive than she'd felt in years.

Seven years, in fact.

She wasn't a girl anymore, and she was much more confident when it came to going after what she wanted. The boundaries Rafael set for their interactions were no longer going to hold her back. This time, *she'd* be the one to make the rules.

"If I do this," she began, her sudden realization of the shift in her power making her feel bold, "if I do come home, it will only be to set up a European office that I can run from London. I have no interest in remaining in California indefinitely. Nor," she added before he could interrupt, "do I have any interest in being a silent partner. I've been boxed up in Papa's house before, trapped and coddled and protected until I thought I'd go mad. I won't do it again." She angled her chin and then moved toward Rafael until *he* was the one to take a step back. "We're either partners in truth, or we aren't partners at all."

"We can work out the details once you get home," he hedged.

"No." She braced her shoulders, knowing that this time, she held more control than he'd ever wish to grant her. She glared at him with the same intensity he'd shown her, the heady shift of power between them bringing a lightness to her chest. "We work them out now or we don't work them out at all."

"I still don't understand why you think this is necessary," Alexander said later that night, after Sophia had told him about Rafael and her father's will. "Your father's dead, Chaves is an overbearing bastard and you have nothing to prove to either of them."

"You're right," she said as she placed her napkin next to her plate. "But you have to admit Raf had some valid points."

"I do?"

"Raf's just following through on a promise." She toyed with the crumpled linen, her thumb tracing a pleat to its monogrammed edge. "And it's what Papa wanted."

"I thought you'd given up trying to please your father when you left California."

"I did. But maybe going back is the only way I'll finally move beyond what happened with him. The winery is part of my past, and I can't just continue to ignore that."

"Why not?"

"Because I'll never know whether this is supposed to be my path if I don't give it a try."

"But you have a path here." Alexander stopped her fidgeting with a warm hand and then waited until she met his concerned gaze. "A perfect path."

"Perfect?" she asked, remembering Rafael's assessment of the predictable boredom of servicing a string of safe, stodgy clients. Her gaze slid left as she contemplated an unending stretch of years spent catering to rigid, inflexible clients who balked at her efforts toward innovation.

"Yes. Perfect. You have a stellar career and you're months away from a full partnership. Why would you throw that all away now?"

"I'm not throwing it all away," she claimed, sliding her hand from beneath his touch. "I'm thinking of this as a new adventure, one in which I'll use everything I've learned here. With the way Raf and I have set it up, I'm actually going to be able to do *more* than I'd ever do here. Besides, if it turns out I hate it, I can always get my position back here."

"Of course you can. You're irreplaceable," he conceded. "But if you leave now, you're also advertising that you aren't fully committed to your career."

"I don't think Wallace sees it that way."

"So you can't see this backfiring on you at all?" he asked, and irritation tainted his tone.

"There's risk in everything," she reminded him while scanning his reddening face. Alex was typically impervious to emotion, and the fact that he seemed almost…*angry* surprised her. "But I can't let the fear of future failures keep me from trying."

"You're moving backward. To a life you hated."

"I didn't hate it."

"You didn't hate *him,* you mean," he clarified, and the accusation stung.

"This has nothing to do with him." She shoved back her chair and stood. She couldn't think with Alexander questioning her, requesting explanations she couldn't give.

"Then what is it?" he persisted.

"I don't know." She strode to the window and stared out into the busy street below Alexander's flat. Unwilling to articulate her reasons aloud, she traced a finger over a misted pane of glass. She hadn't even admitted her reasons to herself. All she'd acknowledged was that her decision was irrevocably tied up with the way she felt about Rafael, her father and the Turino lands. She had unfinished business in California, business she couldn't conduct from her London desk. "It's just something I have to do," she finally said.

"And what about us?"

"Us?" she asked, turning to stare at her good friend while a tendril of trepidation curled low in her stomach. "We'll still be friends. It'll just be more…long-distance."

"I don't want long-distance."

Unwilling to head in the direction he wanted to go, she forced a bright smile. "It's not like we won't have phones or email," she assured him. "And until I set up a European office here, I'm sure business will bring me over at least two or three times a year. We'll see each other plenty."

His mouth firmed as he shook his head. "It's not enough. I'm coming with you. To California."

Her breath caught while she sent him an astonished glance. "Why on earth would you do such a thing?"

"Because I won't abandon you to that man."

"That man?" Sophia laughed aloud, but the sound rang hollow. "I'll grant that Raf's not the friendliest sort, but it's not like he's some sort of monster. Raf would never hurt me."

"Of course he will. You don't see the way he looks at you," he said, and his normally serene features had firmed into an expression of jealousy she'd never seen in him before. "I do."

She blinked and dropped her gaze to her hands, uncomfortable discussing Rafael with anyone, least of all Alexander. "He looks at me like I'm an unwanted obligation he has to fulfill. But he's civilized enough that he won't take it out on me."

"He looks at you as if he means to devour you whole."

"What?" she protested, even as her heart began to pound. "No. You're reading him all wrong. Raf feels nothing but hatred for me. He never has."

"Sophia," Alexander scolded as he gripped her shoulders. "Hatred is the furthest thing from Rafael's mind when he looks at you. Trust me. I'm a man and I know desire when I see it."

Hearing Alexander talk about desire was so horrifically embarrassing that she felt her face heat. "You're wrong. It's nothing like that. Raf and I…we…there is *no* way we'll ever be anything other than partners. I'm a burden, an annoying side effect of his relationship with my father."

Alexander's hands moved to her jaw, tipping her face

until she looked at him again. "Do you know how I know you're wrong?"

Locking her knees to quell the trembling of her legs, she stared at Alexander while dread tightened her chest. *Please don't do this, please don't do this.*

"I know because Chaves looks at you the way *I* look at you."

"Alex—"

"I know. We're colleagues. You don't date coworkers. But you're quitting, right? Now's my chance. And you have to know I've wanted more than friendship from you since the day you were hired on."

"Yes, but I…" She floundered, unable to complete the sentence, she was so uncomfortable. "That doesn't mean you should totally reroute your life just to follow me to California."

A flash of offense darkened his blue gaze. "Are you saying you don't want me to come with you?"

"Of course I…I mean, we're *friends!*" she blurted. "Best friends! But we've never even talked about…about dating and now I'm supposed to be okay with you uprooting your life to follow me?"

"You're not?"

"I don't want anyone making decisions based on what *I* am doing." She pulled free of his touch and backed into the window, resenting that he was pressuring her for more than she wanted to give. "What if it makes you unhappy? What if you hate California?"

"I won't."

"I'd feel guilty that you gave up everything here for a life you'd have never chosen had I not been in the picture."

"But you *are* in the picture, Soph. And being with you is what I want," he said. "Don't you want that, too? Just a little bit?"

A pang of guilt pinched low in her belly. "Alex…"

"Surely you know this is where we've been headed after all this time."

Yes, she had. But she hadn't wanted to confront it. She'd valued his friendship, his company, the easy way they had together. She hadn't wanted the complication of anything more serious, and had been grateful for the excuse of work keeping things platonic. "Alex…I…"

"I know this is sudden, and I know you're not ready to start thinking of us as involved romantically. Not yet. And I wouldn't have even brought it up if you weren't planning to leave."

"I—"

"But you can't deny that we're very well-suited," he persisted as he claimed her hands. "We respect each other, we like each other and we get along famously. Right?"

She flushed and dropped her eyes. "Right."

"I can't think of a better foundation for a relationship. Can you?"

Rather than answer, she allowed him to pull her close, to wrap his long arms around her and lower his mouth to hers. The kiss was warm and gentle, just like Alexander, and its pleasant dampness was a sweet contrast to the voracious plundering she'd experienced with Rafael.

Wanting to enjoy it more, she squeezed her eyes shut and opened her lips. But even as Alexander lingered at her mouth, his tongue gently prodding hers, she felt nothing beyond a detached sense of disappointment. His restraint and patience asked for no more than she was willing to give, and she couldn't help but feel frustrated with his politeness. Just like Alexander, his kiss was…nice. Uncomplicated, respectful and *nice.*

When he pulled back, his face slightly flushed and his breath hitched hard within his chest, as his eyes glittered with fierce intent. "I won't lose you to him, Sophia. I can't."

"You won't," she promised. Of that, she was painfully, irrevocably certain. She lifted both palms to Alexander's dear face and offered a small smile. "But I can't let you come to California. It's too much when I feel so conflicted right now. I value your friendship, I value *you,* and I don't want to lose you. But I'm not ready for this yet. I'm sorry, but I'm just not. I have to resolve things with my past before I can think about a future with you."

CHAPTER SEVEN

A MERE eight days following her return to California, Sophia awoke again at dawn. She dressed in a light pair of khaki pants and a thin white blouse before twisting her hair into a utilitarian knot that kept the curls out of her eyes. Staring out her window at the vineyard, awash in rosy morning light before the heat of the day had descended, she felt the same surge of anticipation she'd felt when she stepped back onto Turino land. *Her* Turino land. The more time she spent here, the more she realized Rafael had been right. Being here, taking her place in the long line of Turino wine makers, *was* her destiny.

Despite Rafael's avoidance of her now that she was home, she'd spent the days reacquainting herself with the land she'd left behind. She'd delivered lunch to the workers yesterday and had met all the new hires who'd joined the vineyard since her time away. She recognized most of them from the funeral, and made a point to ask about their families before leaving them to their duties.

Today, Sophia crept down the main staircase, not wanting to awaken Dolores. She eased the front door open and stepped out onto the tiled patio. Within a hundred yards, she stood between green, shoulder-high rows of twisted vines laden with clumps of chalky blue and plum. She traversed a few of the parallel lines of leaves and fruit and then stopped to select a single plump grape. Pulling it free of its stem, she rubbed her thumb over its dusky flesh until the deep purple hue appeared, shiny from its contact with her skin. It was firm and when she popped the fruit into her mouth, its juice was both sweet and tart.

On impulse, she shed her shoes and socks and then dug her bare toes into the cool, dry earth. Inhaling deeply, she closed her eyes and tilted her face toward the riot of orange and red that gilded the horizon and washed her future livelihood in shades of gilt pink and marigold. The scent of the vineyard was a poignant reminder of the summer days of her childhood, when her entire world had been this stretch of land, these tidy rows of tended vines, the workers that labored for her father and Rafael.

Rafael, who now seemed more distant and bitter than she'd ever thought him capable of being.

Despite the tenuous agreement they'd made, she could tell he wasn't happy having her here. Yes, he'd felt compelled to bring her here for Papa's sake, but he didn't relish having her underfoot. He didn't really care to be her partner or her friend. They'd barely exchanged ten words on the flight back to California, and after they'd landed, she'd almost changed her mind about coming home. Why would she willingly court the conflicts that were sure to come?

But she'd never stopped wondering how things could have been, had he ever allowed her inside.

Which was why she'd come, wasn't it? To pry the secrets of Rafael's past out into the open. To see him as the man he truly was, and to show him the woman she'd become.

Wise or not, rational or not, she fully intended to bring an end to the chapter of her life entitled *Rafael.* She didn't know how it would end and fully expected a bit of a tragic twist, but she was not going to simply stand by and watch things unfold this time. She wouldn't beg for a resolution, but she wouldn't cower from the uncomfortable interactions, either.

She'd experienced a moment of clarity on their flight over as she'd watched Rafael stoically ignore her, his big body tense with suppressed agitation.

The mystery that was Rafael still intrigued her.

He still intrigued her.

And before the chapter ended with him, she intended to bring the tension between them to a head. He could throw up all the walls he wanted; she would not be deterred.

She didn't expect him to love her. She'd never be fool enough to make such a stupid mistake twice. But she'd never, ever stopped wondering what it would be like to peel back the layers that were Rafael and expose the man beneath the protective shell.

Turning, she lifted her eyes to trace the boundary of Turino land. Her stomach took a startled dive when she saw a tall, dark silhouette moving through the adjacent field, and a flutter of recognition went through her as she realized it was Rafael. Just like in the mornings of her youth, the breeze teased his black hair and pressed the front of his white shirt against his chest.

She swallowed and grew still, wondering if she should quietly retreat before he noticed her or force the confrontation they'd been avoiding since her arrival home. But before she could decide, he glanced up from his survey of his plants, and surprise etched his features as he registered her presence. A momentary flare of hunger heated his eyes before he schooled his expression back into its usual mask of black moodiness.

Excitement, along with the shocking realization that she *wanted* this clash, almost twenty years in the making, kept her from turning tail and running. And even as her better judgment screamed at her to scurry for cover, she strode straight toward him as if she expected him to welcome her. *Behave the way a partner behaves,* she reminded herself. *Calm and professional and businesslike.* She pasted a pleasant smile on her face, ignored the pulse winging hard beneath her skin and steadily closed the distance between them.

He wore denims and boots again, his loose white shirt tucked into the waist and the worn spots on his knees, thighs and groin drawing her attention. When she finally reached him, his black gaze tracked her from head to toe, cataloging her wrinkled clothing and her unkempt hair.

"You'll cut your feet," he said darkly, as if his vineyard's rich soil was bristling with knives and broken glass.

"I'll take my chances," she answered with a small smile. He could be moody and mad over nothing, but she refused to sink to his level. Not now, when they had a future to build together.

"Don't you remember your trip to the hospital when you almost lost your little toe?" His scowl held more than a trace of outrage. "Or have you conveniently forgotten that as well?"

"I was twelve," she reminded him. "And being chased by you, if I recall. I've kept an eye out for rogue shovels ever since."

"Put your damn shoes on, Sophia."

"Or what?" she challenged, cocking her head and staring at him with as innocent an expression as she could muster. With Rafael, she'd learned early on to overlook his terse edicts. Otherwise, she'd have spent her life locked up in her bedroom, her only portal to the world a safe, tempered window of glass.

His nostrils flared and a furious tension in his muscles made ropy knots appear in his forearms.

Rather than give him time to fabricate a suitable reply, she switched the subject. “I noticed that Papa no longer bottles Chardonnay. When did that start?”

He shifted restlessly, his reluctance to abandon the topic of her safety as clear as the flexing of his jaw. “Three years ago.”

“And Dolores reports that you split the wine production completely.”

“Yes.”

Monosyllabic replies aside, at least they were conversing in civil tones. She had to celebrate her small successes. “So Papa only made the reds, while you were left with the more challenging whites.” She cocked her head, studying his inscrutable expression. “How’d that work out for you?”

“Fine,” came his curt reply.

Amused, she didn’t allow his grumpiness to dissuade her. “I heard your winery design is quite innovative.”

Obviously uncomfortable with her study of him, he scowled. Again. “Common sense isn’t innovation.”

Sophia turned to view the three-story winery that had been erected in her absence, its clean, rustic lines set seamlessly into the hill at the center of Rafael’s property. “I’d love to see it. Will you show it to me?”

Just as she’d anticipated, he met her request with grumbling resistance.

“I know you’re busy,” she said, drawing up close to his side. He tensed at her nearness while she pretended not to notice. “But we’re partners. I have to understand all the workings of our business if I’m to take part in it.”

He shifted his focus to her and frowned. “Fine,” he growled. “But only if you put on your shoes.” He didn’t wait for her before turning on his heel and heading toward the winery, his long strides forcing her to run to catch up.

Once she did, she grinned up at his dark scowl. She maintained a determinedly cheerful stream of chatter despite his stoic silence as they drew closer to the brow of the hill. "I heard you designed an innovative gravity-flow winery that turned the wine-making community on its ear," she said.

"Gravity flow is the best system available." He shifted restlessly to the left, creating space between them. "Everyone already knew that."

"True. But your design is a revolutionary blend of old and new technologies," she said as she moved close yet again. She squinted at the nearly seamless integration of timber and functionality nestled into the existing notch between slope and pasture, and then returned her focus to his averted profile. "And it's as visually inconspicuous as it's been rumored to be. How did you manage it, and still include all the necessary levels?"

"We just determined where the most cost-effective use of gravity could be used," he said without turning. "And ensured we had adequate space to handle the critical early stages of wine-making."

She nodded and reached for him, stalling his forward movement. "From what Dolores tells me, there was no *we* involved." Sophia cocked her head and smiled as she squeezed his hard wrist. "She said you had to hire eight different architects before you finally found one willing to build to the specs you designed."

His jaw flexed and he tugged free of her touch. "There weren't many professionals willing to align their reputations on architectural plans some nobody from the streets dreamed up."

Hating that he spoke of himself that way, she wanted

to protest that he wasn't a nobody. He never had been, no matter what had happened to him in the past. Even when she'd first met him, when he'd been wounded, bruised and more skittish than a creature brought in from the wild, she'd sensed the value and worth of the hurting boy within.

She'd wanted to wrap her arms around him and *show* him that he deserved a life filled with beauty and joy. No matter what he said, no matter what he did, she knew, down to her soul, that beneath the hardened shell of an impervious, solitary male, Rafael possessed a rare, vulnerable heart. A heart she *still* wanted to heal. "Tell me about how you solved the problem of grape delivery from different lots," she said instead.

"People make more of it than it is," he grumbled as they stepped into the fermenter room with its complex network of stainless sorting flats, forklifts and cranes. "We just had to use a conveyor belt that could run in two directions."

She stifled a smile, not at all surprised by his modesty. "And a turntable that completely eliminated the need for a mezzanine level."

He frowned, rejecting her flattery. "I didn't want to take the entire platform outside just to turn it around."

"Nor did you want to take it outside to clean it."

He didn't seem to appreciate her observation and remained silent as he guided her down to the level where the settling tanks were housed.

"The lab is on this level, too, right?" she asked, craning her neck to see its location midway between the barrel and fermentation rooms.

"Yes."

She resisted his efforts to rush the tour, slowing to admire the three-story circulation spine flanked by several large skylights and catwalk bridges. "It's much lighter in here than in Papa's winery." She turned a slow circle, marveling at the way the interior design connected all the major spaces of the building. "I love how it's both beautiful and functional. And those buttresses are genius."

He offered no response as he steered her down onto the lowest level and its four vaulted rooms. Gravel floors, open to the soil below and flanked by concrete walkways with independent heating and cooling systems, lent an industrial flavor to the cave-like spaces filled with row upon row of wooden casks.

"Why is this room empty?" she asked at the last cavernous room lit by slanting morning light.

He turned to face her, blocking the entrance while amber light cast his face in shadow. "This is where we store our orders before shipping. We're in between shipments right now."

She nodded and turned to survey the empty room, glinting with tiny filaments of light and rich with the aroma of oak and wine. "Dolores tells me Papa was very proud of your design. He never stopped talking about it."

"Your father loved having the Turino name bandied about in the news," Rafael said. "As much as he claimed otherwise, I think he enjoyed being famous."

"I believe you're right," she told him, cocking her head and studying him with a soft smile. "Thank you."

He stared at her for a long moment and she felt heat coil deep in her stomach. "I didn't do it for you," he finally said, as if he were trying to push her away, trying to ruin the small sliver of peace they'd found.

"I know. But you made him proud when I couldn't," she said. "You gave him moments of happiness and joy, and I'm grateful for that."

"Your father deserved to be happy," he said. "He was a good man."

"So are you," she reminded him, wishing he'd realize that he, too, warranted some happiness in his life.

"The tour's over," he told her, while his mouth settled into its typical grim lines of rebuttal. "And I have work to do."

Of course he did. He always preferred solitary work over conversation. So she ignored his blatant dismissal. "How long will it take, do you think, before you consider your debt to Papa cleared? Before you can build a life for yourself instead of for him?"

He glared at her while she stared at him expectantly.

"A year? Ten years? The rest of your life? What?" she prodded.

"None of your business."

"None of my business!" she repeated. "How can you say that when I'm supposed to be your partner?"

For several long moments, he didn't answer her. Instead, he simply stared at her until she felt her breath grow shallow. Twining her hands together at her waist, she felt her courage start to falter. When it lost its foothold altogether, she dropped her gaze to his chest and wished she hadn't brought up the subject in the first place. He always made her feel like an interloper, like a child who'd forgotten her manners.

"Why does it matter so much?" he finally asked in a low, intense voice.

She lifted her gaze to find him looking at her, and the fierceness with which he asked the question made a small shiver chase down her spine. "Because the way you're looking at me makes me think *I'm* the debt you have to pay. And I don't want to be a debt for you."

"You're not a debt. You're—" He interrupted himself and then dragged a hand over his mouth. "Look. I made a promise to your father, and I'd go to the grave before I broke it."

"Which is my point exactly." It shouldn't have surprised her, considering the fact that were it not for Papa, Rafael would most assuredly be dead. Or worse. She still remembered the first time she'd seen him, his bloody feet, matted black hair and bruised, wounded body providing such a stark contrast to Papa's white sheets. "I'm here because of a promise. Not because you want me here."

"I never said—"

"I know. But I hate how it feels like we're both my father's prisoners. It felt like that the first time I left, and it's certainly not the reason I agreed to return."

"Then why did you return?"

"You mean other than the fact that you were blackmailing me?" She shook her head, gathering her courage, and then finally broached the subject she'd been avoiding for far, far too long. She'd never stopped wondering about the terrors he must have survived before coming to the Turino estate. She'd never stopped wanting to somehow mend the terrible scars of his past, to bring him peace. "I came home because I wanted closure." She swallowed, knowing she was bringing things to a head far more quickly than she ought. But she never was one for half measures, and she'd never been known for her overt sense of caution. "I wanted closure with you."

"Me?"

"Yes..." She wished he trusted her enough to share his secrets with her, to unburden the weight upon his soul that kept him so grim and alone. "I want to know *you,* Raf. I want to help you be happy."

"No," he murmured, taking a step away from her and presenting his back. "You don't."

"I do," she insisted as she circled his averted body to

face his taut profile. "I want to know what happened to you, before you came here. I want to know why you feel like you owe your life to Papa, and why nothing you ever do is enough."

A muscle flexed in his jaw. "No."

She moved closer, ducking until their eyes met once again. "If we're going to work together, if we're going to be partners, you have to be open with me. I can't be partners with a stranger."

His black eyes remained fastened on hers, though the pulse in his temple visibly throbbed. "You don't need to know my past to be my partner. Your father accepted that. You should, too."

"Why don't you want me to know you?"

He answered her with silence, until she reached for the bare, browned forearm that hung in tense stillness at his side.

"Raf," she said softly, "if your past keeps you locked up and unhappy, if it keeps you from communicating properly with me, then this partnership can't work. I'm not my father. I need to *know* you. If I don't, it handicaps you and our ability to work together."

The muscles flexed beneath her fingers, but he allowed her touch. "It handicaps *you,* not me. Not everyone needs to advertise their history to function successfully in the world."

"Is that what you call this? Functioning successfully?"

"Yes."

"When's the last time you were happy, Raf? Truly, blindly, can't-stop-smiling happy?"

"I fail to see what that has to do with anything," he muttered.

"Of course you do. This partnership, this winery and *me,* we can't be your penance. It's not right." When he didn't respond, she waded further into the uncharted waters and murky depths of the man whose history had intrigued her for her entire life. "I can't be your partner unless you *want* me to be."

"I do," he growled.

A quick glance at his grim face told her he lied.

"A deathbed promise to my father isn't enough of a reason for us to be partners, Raf. I want more and you deserve more."

She could tell from his expression that he didn't like her knowing anything about his motives. Nor did he like her making assumptions about his character.

"You deserve happiness, Raf," she persisted. "Despite everything, you're a good man. I know it. Dolores knows it. What's it going to take for you to know it, too?"

Rafael stopped breathing, his muscles going still as stone beneath her fingers.

"Bringing me here, sharing your business with me, is not a sentence you need to pay. Not if you don't want to."

"You belong here." His voice was so low she almost didn't hear.

"Not nearly as much as you do." Her grip upon his warm forearm tightened as she waited for his obsidian eyes to meet hers. "So why don't you tell me how to make this easier for you? Tell me what I can do to make you happy."

"You can't," he said. "No one can." The intensity of his rough words sent a spiral of unease through her belly.

"Why?" she insisted. "Why won't you let anyone in?"

He dragged his arm from her fingers and withdrew two steps. "Because I function better on my own."

His rejection stung, but she'd expected it. He always lashed out when she veered too close. "How do you know, when you've never tried it any other way?"

"I told you I have work to do," he said instead of answering.

"Then let me help you," she said, hoping it would stall his retreat. "Let me be the partner I want to be."

"Damn it, Sophia. I told you our partnership wouldn't work that way. You're—" He cut himself off, jerking his head to the side and clamping his mouth shut. As much as he preferred to appear unruffled by the change in their circumstances, promising to bring her back when he so obviously wished otherwise unnerved him.

"I'm what?" she persisted. A stolen glance at his expression told her he didn't like being pushed to answer. But when had he ever? His preference, always, was to live, breathe and think alone. There was safety in solitude and space, but she never had been good at giving it to him. "A pesky little child? A girl who never knows when to keep her big mouth shut? A woman who refuses to respect your boundaries?"

"Yes."

"Yes?" she asked.

When he didn't clarify, she answered for him. "It's a jumble, isn't it?" she said with a wry half smile. "There's so much history between us, so many expectations and misunderstandings, it's a wonder we can make sense of any of it."

He didn't reply, merely glared at her with that same exasperating mulishness as before.

"I own half the vineyard now," she told him. "We share a business and if we're to remain successful, we can't be estranged. I need you to help me learn how to do my share. You have to find a way to treat me as the partner I am."

"I realize that."

"Then stop treating me like a child who needs watching. Stop treating me like the girl I was seven years ago."

He frowned and then grumbled something about her being rash and spoiled and impetuous.

Sophia shook her head and sighed. "Yes, I'm impetuous at times. But I'm not the same Sophia you remember. I've grown up. At some point, you'll have to accept that I'm a woman, capable of contributing something worthwhile to the world and to our shared business."

His pupils dilated while his nostrils flared. "I've known you're a woman for ten years, Sophia."

Rafael's confession sent a tight tangle of conflicting emotions spiraling through Sophia's belly. Desire, frustration, a scared bid for self-preservation and anticipation all warred within her, making her breath catch in her throat. "You don't act like it."

Quick as lightning, he stepped forward to grip her shoulders between his wide, warm hands. "Then how should I act?"

"I—I don't know," she stammered, her heart clubbing hard in her chest. "You certainly shouldn't be keeping secrets from me or lecturing me when I take off my shoes."

His hands moved to the sides of her neck, his strong fingers bracketing her skull and tipping her face toward his. "What, then? Should I be trying to seduce you?" His black eyes were as flinty as stone. "Telling you I want you in my bed?"

She pushed against his chest, but his hold on her didn't relent. "N-no. Of course not."

He dipped his head and breathed against her lips. "That I want your skin against mine?"

A stunned inhale claimed whatever reply she might have made.

"That thoughts of you drag my nights to hell and back?"

Sophia felt her pulse everywhere: in her hands, her maligned feet, her quivering knees. He lowered his face that last disastrous inch and brushed his mouth over hers. The tip of his tongue traversed the seam of her lips and a current of desire flooded her veins. Her common sense reminded her that she should push him away, that she should reestablish the boundaries of their partnership. But she couldn't. With his mouth scalding hot against hers, his tongue demanding entry and his hands hauling her up hard against his bowed body, she lost her will to resist.

She wanted to regain the upper hand, to put him in his place until they'd had a rational, *reasonable* exchange. Even as she arched against him, looped her hands over his warm neck and met his fiery kiss with the same dizzying passion as before, she wanted to win. His big hands gentled against the base of her spine and then slid up, beneath the loose, fluttering edge of her blouse. She felt the light exploration of his fingers along the small of her back, the faint caress of his calloused fingertips against her bare skin. He trailed soft strokes up her sides, his warm palms flattening against her ribs and the tender transition from underarm to breast. Her stomach tightened and her nipples drew up into hard, aching knots. She wanted him to touch her there.

She wanted him to lay her down in the musty darkness and finish what they'd started so many years ago.

Her hands fluttered to the back of his head, to the silky, soft hair that was as dark as ink, and then she leaned forward to press her breasts against his chest, to ease the ache that centered at their distended tips.

His fingers slid south again, his hands curving over her buttocks as he hauled her flush against the long, hard bulge that strained against his denims.

She moaned and rocked against him before the sound of approaching workers brought a moment of sanity. She tore her mouth from his while embarrassment and shame made her chest seize. He'd been trying to illustrate his point, to derail her from her bid to know him, and she'd responded with the same mindless abandon of before. Did she possess no control at all? He didn't even want her! He'd merely learned which arsenal of tools to use on her to get what he wanted.

Mortified that she'd allowed him to completely silence her with nothing more than a kiss, she shoved at him with both hands. After a moment, he released her and his hands dropped to his sides. She couldn't bear to look at him, to see the subtle triumph beneath his hooded, watchful gaze.

"Go home, Princess, before you get hurt," he said before turning on his heel and striding toward the tribe of workers who were gathering at the entrance to the sorting level.

She stood in stunned, angry silence, battling the longing and frustration that still pumped hard within her veins. She was a fool. A blind, cocky fool. And knowing how far in over her head she was, she realized she should have never, ever come home. But she couldn't quit now. She couldn't admit defeat when she'd barely begun. She wouldn't give Rafael the satisfaction of putting her in her place without him having budged an inch.

No. She was stronger than this.

Squaring her shoulders and lifting her chin, she exited the barrel room and looked up at the workers who'd arrived. *Their* workers. She donned a mantle of friendly professionalism and climbed toward the knot of men, determined to show Rafael that she was just as unruffled by what had transpired as he.

Extending her hand, she smiled at the first man she'd seen enter the winery. He wasn't much taller than she, was built like a wine cask and possessed a wide, white grin.

"Hello," she said. "I'm Dante's daughter and Rafael's new partner, Sophia."

He accepted her hand and his smile grew even wider. "Nice to meet you, Miss Turino. I'm Manuel, and my sons, they are Carlos, Jose and Rodrigo."

She felt Rafael's hot gaze on her profile, but she ignored him as she shook each of their hands in turn. "I take it you and your sons are partially responsible for the success of Turino wines?"

He bobbed his dark head. "*Sí.* We follow Mr. Chaves's instructions, and the wines sell very well."

"So Rafael is a good boss, I take it?"

"Sophia," Rafael interrupted with a warning tone.

"I want to hear about your managerial style," she said brightly, turning to him with a wide smile. She looked up into his intense face, her face carefully devoid of any emotion that might lead him to believe his kiss had disturbed her.

"You don't need to hear about my management style," he said with a dark frown. "That's not your role here. Remember?"

Sophia turned to find the workers listening to their exchange with undisguised interest. "Will you excuse us, please?" She looped a hand around Rafael's hard bicep and smiled at their employees. "Rafael and I apparently still need to do a bit of negotiation regarding this partnership of ours."

Rafael's arm flexed beneath her fingers, but his expression didn't change. "Start with the five north rows," he told them.

When the men were out of earshot, he withdrew his arm with a yank and then turned to Sophia with a glower. "Need I remind you that this is *not* what we agreed to? You were to work on advertising and developing additional overseas markets while I continued the roles I've always fulfilled. You aren't to pester the workers for details about me."

"Worried about what I'll discover?"

His scowl deepened. "Not at all."

"Then what's the problem?"

"You're overstepping."

"I'm making you uncomfortable, you mean."

"Call it whatever you want. You shouldn't be here, distracting my men. You know how to craft a brand that will sell in Europe. So go do that and leave me to my work. Now."

"I wish it were that easy."

"You should be as busy as I am. Marketing and advertising were your jobs in London, and from what I've heard, you were quite good at it. You don't get that way if you don't work at it."

"What makes you think I'm not working right now?"

He exhaled noisily. "Look. We agreed that I wouldn't interfere with how you do your marketing job if you didn't interfere with my wine production side of things."

"Did we? Odd, but I don't remember it that way."

"Soph—"

"How about you don't try to box me in the way you promised not to do?"

"I'm not boxing you in. I'm merely keeping you from jeopardizing everything your father worked so hard to build."

"You're boxing me in."

"While you're trying to involve yourself in things that don't concern you."

"No. You're not holding up your end of the bargain, when you promised you would," she accused.

"I said I'd give you whatever you needed to help open up the overseas markets to our brand. And I've done that."

"I can't develop a marketing plan for our business in a vacuum. I have to know the business from the inside out."

"You already know its history and I gave you the past seven years' worth of books to peruse. You can't possibly need more than that."

"Of course I do! Our future consumers won't care about the dry, boring numbers generated by the Turino Winery. They want an emotional connection. A story. And I can't give it to them until I can articulate the human element of this company."

"Consumers won't care about some glorified *story* you concoct."

"You're absolutely right. If the story and the emotion are not authentic, the consumers will know and it'll hurt our sales."

"They don't need a story at all. The quality of Turino wines speaks for itself, just as it has for the past two hundred years."

"Do you want to expand our European market share or not?"

A glare was his only response.

"I can't craft an updated brand for Turino wines that will impact our sales without knowing *you* first."

His nostrils flared with his inhale, and she could tell his hold on his patience was slipping. "That's ridiculous. Did you *know* O'Toole from O'Toole Refrigeration before you drew up his plan?"

"Yes. As a matter of fact, I did." She crossed her arms and jutted her chin toward him. "I learned all about how Richard O'Toole grew up, how he struggled to support his ailing mother while going to school and working two jobs, how he met his lovely wife and how it was she who convinced him to open his own business when they were living on less than ten pounds a week."

Raf's expression darkened even more with his scowl. "You don't need all that to sell refrigeration."

"Now who's telling whom how to do her job?" she shot back. "That's part of what makes me so good at what I do. I make it personal. Consumers react to the stories. Even if I only hint at something personal, something intimate, it will attract them to the brand I'm creating."

His onyx eyes smoldered with a flame she couldn't seem to stop herself from stoking. She wanted his guard to slip, she *wanted* to pry beneath his steel barriers until they finally cracked. If she had to use the excuse of business to do it, then so be it.

So when he stepped toward her, moving until he loomed over her with a menace she knew was all for show, she cocked her head back and dared, "Silence me with kisses all you want, I won't stop asking until you answer my questions."

"I have no intention of kissing you again," he growled.

Knowing he lied and reading the frustrated desire in his expression, a shiver of anticipation shot through her veins. "I'm glad to hear it," she goaded. "Because I have no intention of kissing you, either. It makes it very difficult to carry on a decent conversation."

His angry silence made it even more difficult.

"So tell me, Raf," she prodded, "what's *your* story?"

When he remained stubbornly, maddeningly quiet, she shrugged. "You do realize, don't you, that I won't give up. I'm much more resilient than I was seven years ago."

"Then you'll spend a lot of time being frustrated," he said roughly.

"Fortunately, it's a state I've grown quite accustomed to handling," she mused with a wry smile.

His gaze flicked to her mouth, her breasts, and then back to her eyes. "Somehow, I doubt it."

A blush heated her from her toes to her hairline, but she didn't allow it to derail her. "At some point, you'll accept the fact that you don't always get what you want, Rafael. You'll let down your guard and let me in. For the good of the business and what you owe my father, you'll stop this ridiculous stonewalling and behave like a rational man."

CHAPTER EIGHT

THEIR standoff lasted another two weeks, until Sophia realized she'd overestimated her resilience and underestimated Rafael's ability to stand his ground. No matter what tactic she tried, Rafael remained stubbornly distant, harsh and unreachable. He hadn't kissed her again, hadn't talked to her, and the tension between them seemed more pronounced than ever before. Her inability to chip beneath his defenses, his constant, unrelenting rejection and his coldness had eroded whatever confidence she'd gained in her seven years away from home.

She couldn't do this. She couldn't pretend that his blatant dismissal of her didn't hurt. Yes, she loved the Turino lands and its tribe of seasonal workers. Yes, she'd missed the daily communion with sun-drenched soil, cool morning breezes and ripening vines. But it wasn't enough. Having wine-making in her blood, her father's legacy to protect and the sun at her back wasn't enough to counteract the daily rejection she faced with Rafael. It didn't ease the aching turmoil in her heart.

She'd wanted to connect with Rafael again, to touch some part of his guarded soul. And he'd refused her. Only this time, he'd refused more than just a childish protestation of love. He'd refused *her.*

It hurt more than she cared to admit, and it reminded her

of all the reasons she'd left in the first place. It reminded her of why London and Alex's safe, dependable adoration were so much better.

So it was with a heavy heart that she knocked on his door the following evening. "You win," she told him the moment he opened his wide, hand-carved door. "I'm returning to London."

A flash of dark refusal lit his black eyes.

"My flight leaves in the morning," she said before he could forbid her to go.

"You can't leave."

"I'm not abandoning the Turino legacy, so you needn't fret about your promise to Papa," she assured him. "I told you that I wanted to set up a European office to coordinate our overseas sales, and I'm ready to do that now."

"But we don't have enough European business to justify the expense yet."

"We will," she assured him. "I've arranged a reception to host London's premier restaurateurs, and I'm confident that the business I garner there will generate more than enough revenue to warrant my relocation."

"No," he said roughly. "We aren't ready."

"After the reception, we will be. And since we already have the capacity to increase production, and our distribution channels are in place, all that's left is putting them into operation. It'll take a week or two at the most."

"No."

"Yes, Raf. We're partners. And it's obvious I can't be your partner here. You refuse to communicate with me and you sabotage my efforts to become involved in the day-to-day operation of the winery. It's clear that my presence here is not needed, and staying in California when I'm so obviously irrelevant is not only a waste of my time, it's bad for business."

"You can't go. I won't allow it."

"I wasn't asking permission," she told him while she straightened her spine and forced herself to meet his eyes without quailing. "I'm a full partner and I've decided to start acting like one."

Rafael followed her to London, which surprised her and set her nerves on edge. He'd bumped their flights up to first class, telling her she was not allowed to travel in coach. But just when she was foolish enough to think they'd be able to spend the transatlantic flight easing some of the tension between them, he'd pulled out his laptop and put that fantasy to rest.

He'd worked the entire flight, taking only the occasional break to eat. Aside from the accidental brush of his forearm against hers, or the inadvertent bump of a stray knee, she may as well have been a piece of furniture.

"I upgraded the reservations you made," he later told her as their limousine pulled up to the Berkeley Hotel. "You're in a corner suite on the top floor."

"You didn't have to do that," she said. "I'm perfectly content in a standard room."

He didn't deign to comment, choosing instead to exit the limousine. He rounded its black trunk, spoke to the chauffeur and bellboy about their luggage and then materialized at her door before she'd had a chance to gather her things.

"You didn't change the conference room reservation, did you?" she asked as she exited the limousine and then straightened to her feet. "I'm pretty sure it's impossible to upgrade those."

"No."

"Good." She'd dressed for the flight, in comfortable taupe linen and cotton, but she was wrinkled and horrifically tense from the close quarters with Rafael. She needed space to collect herself and time to freshen up before the party.

"What time is the reception?" he asked as he escorted her into the lobby. The impersonal touch of his big hand at the base of her spine distracted her at the same time that it made her wonder if she'd simply imagined the kisses they'd shared less than a month ago. If she didn't know better, she'd think the passion that had flared between them was a figment of her fevered imagination.

"You don't have to come tonight," she assured him as she eased away from his touch and then rolled her luggage between them. She couldn't think properly with him touching her as if it didn't matter. As if *she* didn't matter. "I know you hate these kinds of things."

"Yes. But I'll be there anyway."

She didn't want him at the reception. Being near him while he ignored her, or worse, treated her with polite detachment, made her feel nervous and distracted. If this night were to work, she needed to be focused. She needed to charm. Rafael's brooding, foreboding presence would undoubtedly derail her from her plans for the evening. She didn't have the emotional resources to shine publicly while worrying about his perceptions of her. "I've worked plenty of clients' parties without incident," she told him. "I promise, you don't need to be there."

"I'm coming."

"You'll hate it," she warned him.

"Did you invite Bennett?" he asked as he collected their keys and strode toward the elevator.

For reasons she didn't wish to explore, Sophia hadn't even alerted Alexander to her presence in the city. "No. Tonight's about business. I don't want to be distracted."

* * *

Rafael escaped to his own room, his control teetering on the edge. He closed the door behind him, his hand gripping tight around the handle while he battled the urge to walk back to Sophia's suite down the hall. The aching throb in his groin, brought about by the unexpected closeness of the elevator, by her intoxicating scent and the way it had filled the small space, whispered at him to relinquish the fight, to lose himself in the wonder that was Sophia.

No.

He knew, if he wanted, he could go to the hotel bar and pick up someone willing and ready. He could relieve his physical ache with some random blonde with blue eyes, white thighs and a come-hither smile. But experience had taught him that a few moments of mindless release with someone he didn't care about wouldn't solve his problem. His problem was Sophia. It had always been Sophia.

Sophia, with her infuriating ability to get beneath his skin. To make him want what he could never have.

You don't always get what you want, she'd told him.

Wasn't that the truth?

So why did you follow her to London? Why are you torturing yourself?

It was a question he didn't want to answer. Couldn't answer. From the moment he'd awakened to find her in Turino's office, her tumbled curls in disarray and her perfect breasts unbound beneath that thin white T-shirt, he'd been derailed. One touch of her sweet, pink mouth, and his ability to keep himself separate from her had vanished.

Again.

Rafael looked down at his hands, at the rough hands that were scarred from a life lived in the streets and on the field. He was a nobody. Capable of bringing only pain to those he cared about. So what was he doing here? Why had he come?

When he'd kissed her in the cellar of his winery, he'd told himself it was to scare her, to remind her that she didn't know him and couldn't trust him. He'd kissed her to prove that he wasn't the man for her. She'd believed him, too, scuttling back and staring at him as if he'd somehow tainted her with his touch.

But then she'd rallied, displaying the strength and resilience she never lost, no matter how often he pushed her away. It had taken all his will to maintain his distance, to resist her persistent bid for closeness. And he told himself it was for the best.

He had to keep his impulses in check, to keep her at arm's length, no matter how it wounded her and made her wide blue eyes fill with hurt and self-doubt. Having her defenses up kept him from seducing soft moans from her arched throat, from skimming his lips over the tight, ruched tips of her breasts while she clutched at his shoulders and begged for more.

He dropped his forehead against the door and closed his eyes, cursing his damned weakness. One look from her, and he couldn't think beyond hauling her close, touching every soft inch of skin with his lips and tongue and hands, consuming the sweet scent from her neck and mouth.

Though he doubted Turino had intended it, the terms of his will had crafted an unbearable hell for his valued protégé. By bringing Sophia back home, Rafael was caught in a purgatory from which there was no escape.

And yet if she left, if he allowed her to remain in London permanently, he'd be confined to a hell he knew all too well. He was terrified of the man he would become once she left him again, even though having her close was killing him by slow degrees.

It was killing them both, and he was a bastard for wanting to consign her to purgatory with him.

But how could he let her go? How would he ever survive losing her again?

He'd always been good at separating what he deserved from the things he couldn't have. He knew his place in the world, and had convinced himself that it was enough. He was content. But with Sophia, he lost perspective. He wasn't good enough for her, but he couldn't move past his irrational obsession with her. He couldn't escape the torture of her nearness. But he couldn't tolerate the pain of having her gone, either.

Hell, things could never work between them, and he was a fool to keep the fantasy alive. She was too refined, raised with the world at her feet, a princess who knew nothing of hunger or want. They came from such different places, his dark to her light, that any sort of communion between them was impossible.

But when it came to Sophia, rational thought had no impact. He wanted her. He wanted to catch her head between his palms, kiss her soft mouth and feed on her sweetness until the craving finally went away. He wanted to drag her to his bed, strip her down to nothing but softness and light and lose himself between her welcoming thighs.

He couldn't remember a time when he hadn't wanted her, when he hadn't been driven by the need to keep her close. The summer she'd turned sixteen, when her year away at school had transformed her from a child to a woman, he'd felt poleaxed by his unexpected desire for her. From that moment on, his nights had been filled with painful, aching fantasies from which there was no release, his days with furtive, stolen glances at the woman he could never have.

Swearing beneath his breath, he spun on his heel and strode to the minibar. A stiff shot of Scotch did little to help his mood, but it blunted the edge of his desire. It granted him a semblance of reason. Yes, he wanted Sophia. Yes, his body reacted whenever she was in the same room. It didn't mean he had to act on it. He could keep himself in check. He might not be able to control his feelings, but he could control his behavior. He could keep his distance.

He owed her that, at least. The second swallow of Scotch heated his gut while he stared out at London's skyline. He'd vowed to protect Sophia, to keep her safe from the evils of the world.

To keep her safe from him.

He needed to stay away from Sophia Turino. Partner or not, having her near was playing with fire.

If he didn't allow her to widen the distance between them, if he didn't allow her to leave, it would burn them both.

CHAPTER NINE

THE event Sophia staged for London's premier restaurant owners promised to be a raging success. Attendance surpassed her hopes, Turino wines flowed freely and the excellent musicians she'd hired provided the perfect backdrop of subtle, expansive harmonies. She'd dressed in a sleeveless gold sheath with a boned bodice and fitted skirt, lots of gold jewelry and matching high-heeled sandals. It wasn't the most comfortable outfit, but with her hair up in a French twist and understated makeup that highlighted her eyes, she felt elegant, beautiful and confident.

If Rafael's reaction were any indication, she'd chosen her clothing well. The moment he saw her, his expression transformed from glowering to shell-shocked. For several endless seconds, his gaze had tracked from her coral-tipped toes, up her bare legs to the high hem of gold, to her loose chignon. He'd lingered for one suspended moment at her breasts, pressed high within the corseted bodice, before finally lifting his gaze to hers.

Deep within his onyx eyes, a hot flame of awareness burned. Her body responded with swift shivers, the small hairs at her nape rising and her pulse galloping into an uneven beat. It took supreme effort for her to recall the evening's purpose, for her to drag her eyes away and feign composure.

"Are you ready to be entertaining and engaging?" she asked as she swiveled to survey the throng of prospective patrons. The venue she'd rented offered a glittering view of the city and enough space for the crowd to mingle without feeling claustrophobic. It was a perfect combination of elegance and contemporary chic.

"I hate parties," he growled, tugging at the snowy white collar of his tuxedo.

"Then why did you come?" she quipped, lifting one brow.

His only response was a disgruntled glare.

Determined to make a success of the evening, she ignored his mood and left his side to circulate.

It should have been a wonderful event, filled with ample opportunities to network, converse and entertain. And had Rafael behaved more like a human being than a mulish, overprotective brute, it would have been.

But no. He hovered near Sophia constantly, interfering with every conversation she began and intimidating anyone courageous enough to approach her. On at least five different occasions, she made significant contacts with interested restaurant owners, only to forfeit the prospective sale when Rafael appeared at her side and scowled the grinning males into a quick retreat.

He was compromising possible contracts faster than she could flush them out.

"Are you deliberately trying to sabotage our business efforts?" she hissed at him after his glower had discouraged yet another potential customer from discussing the various wines he wished to acquire.

"We're not going to do business with someone like that," Rafael muttered darkly.

Sophia glared at him. "He coordinates all the wine lists

for five of London's top restaurants. What possible excuse do you have for sending him away?"

"He has shifty eyes."

"Shifty eyes?" She gaped at him, her composure dangling from a swiftly fraying thread. "You can't be serious."

"I don't trust him. And I don't want to do business with him."

"You don't even know him! And I do! He'll do nothing but enhance the marketability and reputation of Turino wines."

He scowled. "Find someone else."

Maintaining her equanimity in the face of his irrationality was becoming more and more of a challenge. "If you're trying to ruin our chances of selling any wine in the entirety of England," she scolded on a whisper, "you're succeeding brilliantly. And personally, I'd like to end the evening with at least one contract so that the entire night isn't wasted."

"Find an acceptable customer, and I won't stand in your way."

"Acceptable!" she blurted, her irritation making her voice slip into an audible range. "They're *all* acceptable, you infuriating beast! I wouldn't have invited them if they weren't!"

When he didn't budge, looking like a slab of irritated, implacable granite, she huffed out an exasperated breath.

"Stay here," she ordered as she left his side. "I'm verifying that the sample tables are restocked. And then I'm circulating. *Don't* follow me."

"Ms. Turino?" asked the handsome and attentive owner of Chez JT, who'd already commented on the superior flavor of their most popular red. "Is it possible to—"

"Of course, Mr. DuBois," she answered before he could

even ask his question. She looped her hand through his arm and beamed up at him. "And please, call me Sophia."

"Will your partner be joining us again?" he asked while casting a worried glance toward the huge, dark and threatening Rafael.

"No. Come. I was just on my way to ensure the whites have been replenished," she said, gesturing toward the stacked cube sculpture and its circle of sample tables residing in the center of the large space. She chattered with Mr. DuBois as they wound their way through the clustered mass of restaurant owners and head chefs. Stealing a glance over her shoulder, she cast a warning look at Rafael, who stared after her with a scowl.

Swallowing back the pressure of a wholly inappropriate laugh, she decided that Rafael Chaves was the most frustrating, infuriating male on the planet. He didn't want her in California, yet was willing to sacrifice the success of their expansion just to keep her from moving to London. It was enough to drive her stark raving mad.

"Have you been in business with Chaves for long?" asked the man as he gestured with his chin back toward Rafael.

"He was my father's partner for years," Sophia said, trying to sound flippant despite her irritation. "His interpersonal skills need a bit of polish, but he's a wizard with the wines. Here," she offered, "try the Pinot Grigio. It's divine."

She felt herself relax as the owner sampled one wine after another, closing his eyes and smiling with unabashed pleasure. By the time he'd finished tasting a fourth slender flute, she knew she'd made serious inroads toward a lucrative contract. A heady rush of success eclipsed her anger and made her feel as effervescent as the finest champagne. "You'll find our prices are very reasonable," she confided, "and we've set up a world-class distribution that will ensure you never have to wait for an order to arrive."

"Excellent," he said as he eyed the other samples on her tray. "And though my head chef prefers to have input on all wine orders, I'm sure he will agree yours are superior. May I send him a bottle of the Sauvignon before we decide?"

"Of course," she said with a smile. "I'll go fetch you one."

She'd almost made it to the kitchen and its supply of fresh bottles when Rafael intercepted her, commandeering her elbow and halting her progress with angry precision. "We're leaving," he ordered. "Now."

Sophia's temper flared. "Absolutely not," she said, yanking her arm free of his grasp. "You may not care about generating new business, but *I* do." She skewered him with a scornful glower. "Now move."

"We don't need this kind of business," he snapped.

The head caterer exited the kitchen and drew to an abrupt halt before them, his eyes flickering from one angry face to the other. "Is everything all right?"

Sophia, who considered herself quite mature when it came to controlling her emotions, felt a crazy impulse to screech her frustration at the top of her lungs. With effort, she forced a pleasant smile to her lips. "Everything's perfect. It's just that Mr. Chaves and I are having a minor disagreement."

The man glanced from Rafael's grim expression to hers. "Are you sure?" he asked slowly.

"Yes." She kept her voice steady despite the temper roiling beneath the surface of her skin. "Could we possibly use your office for a few moments? Mr. Chaves and I need to discuss a few items privately."

"Of course," he hedged. "It's unlocked. You remember where it is?"

"Yes, thank you," she assured him, grateful for the civilized surroundings that kept her from losing her temper altogether. "We won't be long. I promise."

"Take your time," he answered with a wave of his hand. "I'll keep an eye on things out here."

She didn't track the caterer's withdrawal, she was so intent on Rafael. As soon as they were alone, she stalked toward the empty office and with an irritated twist of the doorknob, ripped the door open. Gesturing into its dimly lit interior, she ordered Rafael inside with a furious glare. "What is your problem?" she exclaimed as soon as the door was closed. "I'm trying to build *our* business, and you're doing everything you can to sabotage me! You're being unreasonable and ridiculous and I've had *enough!* You have to stop!"

"*I'm* being ridiculous?" he raged. "You're the one who's trying to rush our expansion to London when we're not ready."

"Not ready?" she repeated on an outraged exhale. "Are you insane? We already bottle enough wine to supply the entire continent, and all that's needed is to solidify the contracts and coordinate the distribution."

"Which you know nothing about," he said, towering over her with a murderous expression tightening his features. "And I won't stand by while you undermine my business' expansion just because you want to return to London now."

Infuriated, Sophia shoved at his chest. "I wouldn't want to return to London if you'd allow me to do *anything* in California. *You're* the one who's undermining *our* business by treating me like an unwanted obligation instead of an asset! *You're* the one who's too stubborn to accept that I might actually bring something to the table, or that a partnership between us could actually work if you'd break down your stupid walls and let me be part of your life!"

"You can't be part of my life!" he thundered.

"Well, you've certainly made that painfully clear!" Anger and frustration blazed through her, sparking a futile desire to hurt him. "And you know what? I'm not going to fight it anymore. I've been trying to scratch my way through your walls, thinking that beneath the shields you hide behind, you have the capacity for reason and warmth. For feeling. But I was wrong. You're incapable of feeling anything but anger and resentment toward me. Your soul is an arctic wasteland, and I'm finished with you. Done."

He moved toward her so swiftly, the breath caught in her throat. His furious expression testified to the way her words had wounded him, to the dark layer of rage she'd exposed. Alarmed, she stumbled back a step. A little shock winnowed through her veins as he seized her in a savage grip.

Jerking her to her toes, he leaned over her. "You think I don't feel?" he asked. "That I'm arctic and cold?"

"Raf—"

"You only think that because I don't allow you to see what's inside." He gave her a little shake, while his eyes flashed like black fire. "Should I give my emotions free reign, you'd never survive. They plague me more than all the fires of hell combined and are a torment I wouldn't wish on my worst enemy."

"I didn't—"

"So don't talk to me about my capacity for warmth. Don't you dare talk to me about *feelings,* because if you felt even one hundredth of what I feel, it'd burn you to ash."

Rafael granted her no time to process the dizzying implications of his confession before he claimed her mouth with a brutal hunger. For an immeasurable span of time, she remained frozen in place, too stunned to do anything but fall apart within his arms. His lips slanted over hers, devouring and demanding and taking, his tongue dancing a drugging invitation against hers. Utterly lost, she sank against him and allowed him inside.

Knowing it was wrong and not caring, she succumbed.

How could she not? She'd never stopped wanting him. Needing him.

Faint and breathless, she reached for his neck, for the sturdy cords of muscle beneath the raw silk of his black hair. Her fingers fluttered helplessly from hairline to collar, unconsciously trying to gentle his savage fervor. And then something schooled the swift tempo of his breathing, and he quieted. Became tender. His fingers trembled as he brushed them over her cheek and brow, his rough palms cradling the sides of her face. Tipping her head back, his voracious hunger eased as he lifted his mouth from hers to skim the crest of her cheeks, her eyelids and the tilted tip of her nose with tiny, nibbling kisses.

His initial drive for closeness had pressed her tight against the door, and she slowly became aware of the chilled surface against her bare upper back. The contrast between cold metal and scalding male made her shiver. Arching beneath him, her head drifted to the side as he fed upon her with a delicate exploration of her throat, the low neckline of her gold dress, the swell of breast and hint of cleavage.

Rafael's hands skimmed along the transition from fabric to skin, the pads of his calloused fingertips brushing faint circles over the straining tips of her corseted breasts. She closed her eyes and arched her back, offering no protest as he pulled at the gilded edge of her bodice with impatient, restless tugs. Like an utter wanton, she moved her hands to help him, yanking at the constraining dress until her breasts tumbled free. He gave a low growl of approval and lifted her to her toes, dipping his head to close his hot mouth over her beaded nipple. She squirmed beneath him, biting her lips to keep from moaning aloud, and hooked one leg over his thigh to draw him closer.

A soft groan of satisfaction accompanied the move, and he reached for her other leg. Before she knew it, he'd lifted her up against the cold door and pinned her with his hips. She felt the heat of his flexed waist between her spread thighs as he brought her breasts level with his slick, wet mouth. He circled one taut, pointed tip with his tongue, sending rivulets of pleasure to her throbbing center. And then he formed her sensitive flesh with one wide hand as he sucked her deep into his mouth. When he withdrew to have his thumb flick over the dampened peak of her breast, she jerked reflexively against the granite plane of his body. His mouth returned to trace heat along her throat, kissing, tasting, soothing, while his fingers continued their dizzying exploration of her nipple. Softly, softly, he pinched and squeezed, rolling the exquisitely tender tip while she struggled for breath and writhed in mindless pleasure.

When everything, everything was tight and yearning, he pulled back enough to look at her from beneath hooded eyes. "Sophia," he groaned in a rough voice. "We shouldn't—"

"We should," she whispered, squirming lower until their hips aligned, and then she kissed him into silence. He returned the kiss, deep and fevered, while an aching desire and emptiness and longing filled her body. She drove her hands beneath the shoulders of his jacket, needing to feel his skin.

"Sophia…" His voice was ragged and his breath heaved between them. His fingers, as if they had a mind of their own, continued to brush delicately over the bare skin of her shoulders, her throat, her arms. "We can't—"

"Hush," she told him, tightening her thighs about his hips and plucking at the jet buttons of his tuxedo shirt. "We can."

He closed his eyes as if he were in pain and his hands moved to her buttocks. Stilling her. But she refused to be stilled. She tipped against him, rocking against the hard ridge of his arousal. He exhaled in an uneven gust while his fingers dug into her flesh, pulling her closer. Closer. She reached to kiss his throat, his neck, the rough landscape of his jaw while her frantic hands yanked his shirt free from his pants. Tension climbed within her while she ran her hands under the warmed cotton and over his bare, burnished flesh. She wanted to forget all the reasons they couldn't be together, to climb inside him and never, ever be apart from him again.

"Not here," he panted into her hair while he ground against her willing flesh. "Anyone could…could walk in…."

She reached blindly for the door handle and twisted the lock into place. "I don't care," she breathed as she returned her hand to his nape. "I just want you. Tell me you want me, too."

"Soph…"

"Say it," she demanded.

"God help me," he whispered as he buried his face against her neck. "I do. It's all I can think about."

A heady thrill went through her at the words. "Then show me," she urged, turning to accept his hot, seeking mouth. "Show me, Raf."

As he kissed her, she felt his hand at the hem of her dress, bunching it tight as he shoved it up over her buttocks. And then his thumb hooked in the waistband of her underwear, tugging at the pale satin until it became clear that her position impeded further progress.

"Wait," she breathed as she straightened her legs and reclaimed her feet. "I'll just…" Wriggling between the door and Rafael and with one hand against his chest for balance, she pushed her underwear down her legs, kicked free of the knot of fabric and then returned to press against him.

His gaze trapped hers while second thoughts crested within their dark depths. "Soph—"

"Shh," she repeated as she reached for his waistband and the hint of bare flesh that disappeared beneath black wool and pressed pleats. She fumbled with the button and zipper and white cotton that kept him from view until he jutted free, hot and hard against her palm.

He sucked in a hiss of breath and caught her hand with his, trapping her questing fingers between their bodies. "Stop," he groaned. "We need to—"

"No." She ignored him, twisting her wrist until she held his smooth, tight circumference within the circle of her fingers. "I've waited long enough already." She squeezed delicately, only to let out a startled squeak when he lifted her off her feet again and pressed her up against the door. The movements brought their intimate flesh together and the plump, silky head of his erection bumped up against her slippery core.

Oh... A moan slipped from her throat, her slick flesh swollen and wanting and pulsing and… *Oh*... An erotic haze robbed her of all additional thought. Operating on pure instinct, she flexed her thighs, lifted her pelvis, and then slowly pressed down onto the hard, long length of him. *This* is what she'd waited for, what she'd wanted for so, so long. To share this elemental act with the one man she'd never stopped wanting. To *feel* him deep inside and to welcome him with an acceptance he'd never before allowed.

"Meu deus—" he gasped on a ragged exhale. "Soph—"

"Shh," she breathed before she lifted back up, sliding higher and higher until she felt the threat of separation. Changing course, she lowered once again, staring into his eyes and holding her breath until she'd taken every tight inch of him within.

She began the slow slide back up before he stopped her retreat with a guttural exhale and a strong grip against her hips. With a groan, he altered the torturous rhythm she'd set and surged upward to touch her womb. He withdrew and then buried himself again, his hands shifting to her bare buttocks while his powerful body pressed her flush against the door. His breath beat between them, heaving in uneven gusts as he set a rhythmic advance and retreat within her breached flesh. Exulting in his surrender, in the pleasure she could read in his strained features, she tightened around him while ripples of bliss began to build.

Soon, her eyes drifted closed while tension climbed. Passion and pleasure bled together, blurring beneath her eyelids and sending tendrils of exquisite bliss along the surface of her skin. Over and over, he moved within her as she arched against him, opening, welcoming, wanting. She moved with his rhythm, faster, faster, until whimpers of need slipped from her throat and her fingernails dug into his shoulders. Her heartbeat pulsed wildly, reverberating noisily in her ears, her fingertips, her legs and arms and stomach and…everywhere. Quivering now, trembles wracked her limbs, shaking her as she fought for breath. For control.

And then rapture seized her, drawing a startled cry from her while wave after wave of ecstasy pulled her up into a white intensity of sensation. Pleasure blinded her as every muscle contracted, spasmed, tugged. The universe narrowed to the two of them, to the hardness she clenched deep within her and the strong arm supporting her trembling torso. She clutched at him, her head thrown back and her mouth gasping for breath while she rode the shudders to completion.

After a few moments, she drifted back to herself and became aware of him, of the tough, sleek muscles beneath her fingers and the fierce, ravenous eyes watching her from within his flushed face. Tenderly, she bent to kiss him, to offer wordless thanks. And then he was moving again. She wrapped herself around him, opening for him and taking all he had to give. Taking and taking and taking. She reveled in the low sounds he made, the building tension in his breath. And then a groan wrenched from deep, deep within his chest, buffeting her cheek and temple. He plunged into her a final time, his body going taut and hard beneath her splayed hands.

Long minutes of silence elapsed, both of them fused together and unwilling to return to what they'd been before. But then he slowly eased out of her, placing her on her feet before him. His black eyes studied hers, guarded and inscrutable, before he dropped his gaze and bent to lift his pants.

Unsure of how to navigate the aftermath of their lovemaking in the strained quiet, she dipped to follow suit. She stepped into her discarded underwear and slid them up over her hips. When she tried to restore order to her disheveled dress, her arms bent awkwardly as she attempted to unfasten the crumpled bodice's pleated zipper.

"Let me," he said in a gruff voice as he turned her to face the door.

Though she'd have thought it impossible for a man to help her dress without touching her, he somehow managed it. And when he was done, when his hands abandoned her and they continued to stand without facing each other, without words, she felt an awful, terrible urge to cry.

"Are you okay?" he finally asked.

She kept herself from sniffing—barely—and chirped, "Of course. Why wouldn't I be?"

"You know why."

A strangled sob clutched her throat, but she swallowed it back. Hard. "I'm fine." No matter how horribly vulnerable and bereft she might feel, she would hang on to her dignity if it killed her.

He tugged against her shoulder, his palm both implacable and warm as he turned her back to face him. "Soph."

"What?" she asked, the brightness of her tone sounding brittle even to her own ears.

"I can't imagine that this is what you had in mind when we came in here."

"Do you hear me complaining?" she managed to say, when what she really wanted to say was that it had been wonderful. Wonderful and awful and confusing and the most intense pleasure of her entire life.

"It was hardly the seduction I'd have planned for you."

"Because a quick, impulsive shag against a door isn't your style?"

"Not with you, it isn't." Darkness claimed his features yet again. "You deserve better than this."

"I wanted this," she said, trying to sound cosmopolitan when she felt anything but. "You were doing me a favor."

"A favor," he repeated.

"Yes."

He studied her in silence for a moment, and then bent to retrieve his jacket and shirt. "I take it you were prepared, then?" he said as he straightened and then threaded his arms through both.

She stared at him blankly, unsure what he meant by *prepared.*

"Protection," he clarified, his hands making swift work of his shirt's black buttons. He scanned her face and his fingers suddenly stilled. "Tell me you're on some kind of birth control."

She felt her face go white as understanding slammed into her. "Raf…"

"Maldição," he muttered.

Feeling inexplicably gauche and embarrassed, she clutched knotted hands to her chest. "I'm sorry. I didn't even think—"

"That makes two of us," he interrupted.

"But if I'd thought—"

"What's done is done." His unreadable gaze granted her no clue as to his thoughts. "We'll deal with the consequences if and when they arrive."

It suddenly felt impossible to breathe.

Rafael straightened his cuffs and adjusted his bow tie, returning once again to the remote, beautiful man she ached to call her own. "Do you have everything?"

Unable to process his question, she simply stared at his chest while the possible implications of their impulsive lovemaking claimed all of her attention. She was smarter than this! She was a modern woman, wasn't she? She'd had sex before, and she'd never forgotten protection. Ever. How could she have been so careless, with Rafael of all people?

"Soph?"

She lifted her eyes to his, her hands lowering to press against her trembling stomach as she frantically counted back two weeks. How could he be so calm when their future, a possible *baby* and an additional Turino *burden* hovered so unpredictably on the horizon?

Silence stretched for what felt like an eternity before he finally said, "Wait here. I'm going to go make your excuses at the party."

Her lungs cramped at the thought of facing all those people and feigning a poise she was light-years from feeling. But if he could behave as if episodes of passionate, unprotected sex in the middle of a hotel kitchen's office were an everyday occurrence, she certainly could as well. "No."

"You're in no shape to go back out there."

"I'm the hostess," she protested as she firmed her chin and forced the quaking from her limbs. "I can't just disappear in the middle of the reception. It'd be bad form."

"You can and you will." His black eyes scanned her tipped face and the tense lines of her shoulders and arms. "I'll tell them you're ill." He paused, a nearly imperceptible flexing of his jaw the only clue to his thoughts. "And it won't be a lie."

Sophia bit her lips and realized he was right. There was no way she could fake it. Not after what they'd done. Not after what *she* had done.

He stared at her for another endless moment, unlocked the door and then slowly opened it. "Don't go anywhere until I come back."

CHAPTER TEN

ONCE he was gone and the door was closed between them, Sophia sucked in several quick breaths in an effort to stem the tide of self-recrimination that washed over her. Rafael had always accused her of being impulsive and rash, of making decisions without regard for the consequences. Tonight proved he was right. One kiss from him, and she'd lost all semblance of control, every last shred of judgment.

Shaking, she smoothed her palms over her gold dress and then opened the door. She peered down the white hall to confirm that no one was present to witness her escape before she scuttled toward the kitchen exit and its adjacent elevator.

By the time she entered her suite, an elegant combination of tall windows, black lacquer furniture and billowing lavender and white cotton, she'd already fashioned a plan to leave, to change her name and simply disappear. If she ended up being pregnant, she'd raise the baby on her own. She'd never force Rafael to assume the repercussions of her reckless choice; she'd never bring another unwanted burden into his life. He'd try to track her down, of course, but only because of the promise he'd made to her father. After a few weeks of not finding her, he'd be relieved. He'd be grateful she was gone.

She went to collect her toiletries, shoving them into her

bag with shaking hands, and then returned to her room. Before she had a chance to open her suitcase, a rap at the door sent her heart into a wild, clubbing beat. She twisted to stare at the tall door, frozen in place and trying to convince herself that she'd imagined the sound.

The rapping escalated to a pounding demand for entry. "Sophia?"

"Go away," she mouthed, though no sound came from her tight throat.

"Open the door."

She placed her toiletry bag atop her suitcase and then inched toward the door on wooden legs, feeling as if she were approaching her own execution. The door handle rattled, and she flinched.

"Damn it, Soph. Let me in."

Her hand trembled as she reached for the handle and pulled it down. She cracked open the door to reveal the man who'd never want her the way she wanted him. "Go away," she told him.

He looked as beautiful as he'd ever looked, his hair rumpled and his black brows lowered into a forbidding line. "I told you to wait for me."

That's all I've ever done.

Rafael pressed his way inside. "We weren't done back there," he said as he backed her into the room and then kicked the door closed with his foot.

Her shoulder tingled where his warm fingers gripped her, and she resisted the urge to close her eyes. To lean into him and beg him to ease her worries. To love her. "We were. There's nothing more to talk about."

His gaze flicked to her mouth, then returned. "I told you that wasn't the seduction I'd have planned for you."

She forced a laugh. Rather than being the dismissive trill she'd wanted, it came out nervous and thin. "Is that supposed to make me think you've planned something different?"

"Yes."

The breath froze in her lungs as she stared at him, trying to read the meaning behind that one cryptic word.

"I want you," he said as he stepped closer, his free hand lifting to the back of her neck. "And before this night is over, I'm going to seduce you the way a woman like you should be seduced. Properly. In a bed. Without that damn dress and without any second thoughts or protests coming between us."

The thought of his warm, naked skin pressed against hers made her stomach flood with warmth. "You're going to seduce me?"

His eyes refused to release hers. "For one night, we're going to forget all the reasons this shouldn't have happened and simply enjoy the way we make each other feel."

"Because the damage has already been done?"

"Exactly."

She debated while second and third and fourth thoughts crowded in on top of one another, a cacophony of desperate yeses. One night. One night of blinding pleasure that only Rafael could provide. She knew she'd regret it, but would she regret it more than what they'd already done? Would the pain of his rejection be any worse? "What happens in the morning?" she asked, not wanting to hear the answer, but needing to know anyway.

"We go back to the way things were. We redraw the lines that should have never been crossed."

"What if I don't like the lines you draw?"

Rather than answer her, he simply tipped her chin, kissed her softly and then withdrew enough to brush a strand of hair behind her ear. The gentle, glancing touch of his fingertips along the curve of her ear sent a shiver along her skin. "Let's not talk about lines tonight."

If she were stronger, she'd have mustered the will to refuse him, to protect herself before she lost her heart to him all over again. But she supposed she'd never reclaimed it, had she? He'd had it all along, and she'd been aimlessly coasting ever since. So why not savor a night of passion before reality reared its ugly head again? Why not steal what little time he was offering before it vanished altogether? Morning would come regardless, no matter which choice she made. "Okay."

He reached for her hand and slowly led her toward the bed. When they reached the tall, wide mattress, he turned her away from him and began to unzip her corseted bodice. She could see their reflection in the inky black glass of the windows, and she watched as he gently unfurled her bodice and allowed the dress to drop over her hips. She hadn't worn a bra beneath the boned fabric, so when the gold dress crumpled around her ankles, she was left clad only in her heels and white satin underwear.

When her hands rose to cover herself, his fingers stalled her efforts. "Don't," he murmured against her hair. "I want to see you." For a long moment, they simply stood that way, their reflected gazes locked in the window overlooking the city. Despite the flush of self-consciousness that turned her skin pink, she forced herself to relax. To give him everything he asked of her and more.

His hands slid from her lax wrists to her hips and then tugged her backward against him. The hard length of his arousal bumped up against her buttocks and he dropped his mouth to the shell of her ear. "You're so beautiful," he breathed, "pink and white and perfect, just like I always knew you would be." One big brown hand moved to splay low against her abdomen while the other rose to cup her breast. Adrift in sensation, her head listed to the side and her eyelids slid closed. Taking advantage of her offering, he leaned to kiss her earlobe and the tender side of her neck. His warm fingers brushed delicately over her nipple while his other hand trailed lower, exploring the inch of skin just above her satin panties. When a single finger dipped beneath the band of elastic, a small whimper escaped her throat.

"I want to remember this," he said as additional fingers joined the first to trail over the intimate curls below.

Her hips jerked, lifting toward his hand, and she felt his smile against her neck.

"Every stolen minute." He stroked lower, deeper, his touch skimming over and around and tantalizingly close to where she wanted it most. When she thought she could bear it no longer, he tenderly nudged one finger just inside and pressed his thumb against the aching bud of need. The combination of heat and thrill, as unexpected as it was new, wrenched a stunned gasp from her.

He immediately stilled, his breath warm against her cheek. "Are you okay?"

Biting her lip and too embarrassed by her own naiveté to look at anything but the neat white comforter, she nodded. Going so slowly, with him fully dressed and their reflections giving her an unfettered view of everything he chose to do, she felt as unsophisticated and clumsy as she'd felt the first time they'd kissed. It was as if she'd never been with a man before and she supposed, in a way, she hadn't. She'd never allowed herself to lower her guard and actually *be* with a man who'd claimed her very soul.

"You sure?" he asked, his voice heavy with concern. "We can stop if you want."

"No. Don't stop," she blurted as she twisted to face his chest. "But I want your clothes off, too." She lifted her hands to his tuxedo shirt and made swift work of its jet studs. "I don't want to be the only one naked," she said as she tugged his shirt free of his pants and then spread it open. The breath caught in her throat when her efforts revealed the muscular expanse of bone and muscle, with its light dusting of black, black hair. After a moment, she remembered that this was real, that she could touch all that warm, bronzed flesh without him calling a halt to her exploration. Greedy and curious now, she ran her palms up the muscled ladder of rib and then over his chest, her fingers combing through his hair and brushing tentatively over the flat brown nipples.

He watched her through slit eyes as she memorized the textures that were so different than her own, not saying a word as she familiarized herself with his exposed torso. When she pressed her palms flat over the wide span of his shoulders and pushed his shirt over the thick expanse of taut muscle and sleek skin, he shrugged his shoulders and shook free of ironed cotton. White and black fluttered to the floor as she systematically stripped him down to his underwear. Enthralled, she trailed her fingers over every new inch of revealed flesh, tracing faint, feathery touches from sternum to bicep, from neck to shoulder blade and spine. He was beautiful, and seeing him with his defenses temporarily set aside brought a lump to her throat.

Long legs, strong and thick with bunched muscle, were slightly lighter in tone than the tanned arms and chest above, and she reveled in knowing she had access to skin the sun rarely saw. Unfounded or not, it made her feel special. Valued. Her fingertips traced the ridge of muscle above his hipbones, the tight skin of his flat abdomen, and then converged at the dark arrow of hair pointing south to a flat band of white elastic. When she dropped her fingertips to the tip of his contained erection, he circled her wrist and reclaimed control.

"Later," he promised as he backed her up against the bed. He dipped his lips to hers, leisurely exploring the recesses of her mouth as he peeled her underwear over the rounded curve of her buttocks. Breaking the kiss, he bent to finish the job, lifting first one foot and then the other until she stood completely naked before him. He boosted her onto the bed and then stepped between her thighs before she had a chance to close them.

Unhurried and gentle, his touch felt different than before. Long, languorous strokes relaxed her muscles and made her eyes drift closed even as warm tingles gained ground deep in her belly. He lingered over her body, tending to each sensitive crease and each scented cove from shoulder to toe. Deep, languid kisses moved from her mouth to her breasts to the soft slope of her stomach. Soon, his fingers were probing lower, stroking and teasing and arousing her clenching interior while her hips shifted and stirred.

"Raf," she said. Her toes curled around the bed frame and she lifted her arms to reach for him, to draw him up until his warm skin pressed hot and firm against hers. "I want you to kiss me."

"All right," he said, and she heard the smile in his voice as he resisted her efforts to move him and then inched his way even lower.

Understanding dawned, bringing a hot flush of excitement with it. Tension, wicked and deep, coiled low within her womb as his mouth skimmed her lowest rib and then trailed south along her stomach. A warm, wet dart of his tongue at her navel made her squirm and brought a bubble of nervous laughter to her throat.

But then her laughter died on a gasp when he settled

his mouth upon her. Reflexively, her thighs tightened and tried to close against his head, but his broad hands held her firm. Spread beneath him, her modesty warring with her arousal, she squeezed her eyes shut and twisted her hands in the crumpled coverlet. "Raf…"

"Shh." He blew against her sensitive flesh, his breath a cool contrast to the heat he'd left behind. "Just let me please you."

And he did. Oh, how he pleased her. White arrows of pleasure, hot and insistent, propelled her up, dissolving her sense of self as separate from him. She surrendered to the blurring haze of arousal, helpless to stop the tide sucking her under. Surrender had never felt so necessary. So fundamentally essential. Infused with heat and filled with a desperate, raw need, she arched beneath him while her hands twisted in the white coverlet. Her heartbeat ricocheted wildly within her chest, her flushed skin, her trembling legs and her heels where they dug into the mattress. Too much, too, too much, she writhed beneath him, lost to everything but the wild, mindless communion between them.

"Raf," she implored. Her hands moved to his dark head, guiding him, begging him as his strong, wet tongue drove her inexorably to the brink. Moaning, she lifted beneath his mouth, joining him in the hot, flicking rhythm he'd set.

Caught in the grip of wrenching pleasure, she groaned as ecstasy seized her. Paralyzing rapture suspended her, stiff and hovering at the peak, until the tension released in an exquisite, pulsing rush. Racked with tremors, she tumbled headlong over the edge, her limbs quaking with hard shudders.

"Sophia…" She heard his voice once the blissful spasms subsided.

Dragging her eyes open, she found Rafael leaning over her, his black gaze locked with hers.

"Look at me," he demanded as he lowered to his elbows and cradled her head between his hands.

So she did, his intense gaze demanding that she not shy away from the intimacy of his touch. Then, in one slow, slick glide, he entered her fully. They inhaled in unison, their awareness of the world distilled down to the single, elemental joining of their bodies. For a long moment, neither of them moved, too caught in the wonder of their union. But then she lifted heavy, languid arms to his ribs and curved her arms and hands over his muscled back. His skin was smooth and sleek beneath her palms, and the breath escaped him in an unsteady rush as he slowly dipped his head to hers. She felt the scrape of his whiskers against her cheek, felt the flexing of his muscles and the tightly reined control as he gradually began to move within her.

Meeting his long, unhurried thrusts without resistance, she opened to him and welcomed him as pleasure mounted once again. She hooked her legs around his thighs, flexing her knees and tipping to take more.

She wanted to take all of him. Everything that he'd see fit to give her.

He lifted his head again to watch her, his eyes glittering with banked passion, and she felt an overwhelming rush of love for her poor, wounded and guarded Rafael. He looked fierce, his hunger and need drawing his beloved features taut. She could tell that now, even now, he wanted to hold himself apart. To hold her at a distance even as he kissed her and touched her and made her world fall apart. So she slid her hands down to his lean, flexing buttocks and curled her fingers over the pumping muscle. She drew him closer, wrapping herself around his trembling body as he incrementally increased his pace within her. She lifted upward to press encouraging kisses against his chest, the thick column of his neck and the bristly ridge of his jaw. Rocking beneath him, she offered her unconditional acceptance while her hands urged his release.

Her movements seemed to impel him to greater heights of pleasure, his pace quickening and his braced arms trembling. And yet still he watched her, his intent gaze never straying from hers until he stiffened between her thighs. Only then did his eyes slide closed. He surged forward, collapsing and shaking against her while her name escaped his throat in a fragmented groan.

CHAPTER ELEVEN

MUCH, much later, they lay in a tangled, sated heap. Knowing the night had exhausted her, Rafael urged Sophia to sleep. "Rest," he murmured against her soft hair as he slowly stroked her back from nape to hip. He allowed himself to kiss her again, to trace the fine line of her brow and the sweet bridge of her nose with his lips. His fingers trailed back up along the knobby length of spine, and it occurred to him that he'd yet to chart every inch of her back, to explore the gentle curve of bone and skin, the narrow planes of shoulder blade and the delicate dimples at the base of her spine. *Later,* he told himself as he returned his hand to the notch in her waist. *After she's had a moment to rest.*

"I don't want to go to sleep," she said in a drowsy hum as she nestled closer. She flung a leg over his hip, her fleecy curls brushing intimately against him while her fingers transcribed soft circles over his side. "I don't want to waste a minute of this night."

He felt himself harden again, a throbbing, live eagerness that had nothing to do with respite and everything to do with Sophia. "You're exhausted," he admonished her, even as he vowed to remain awake just to watch her sleep. Somehow, the need to infuse every moment with full awareness banished his fatigue, filling him with a desperate desire to hold her, to watch over her and to imprint each minute in his memory as necessary and distinct.

"Mmm," she agreed drowsily as her hand moved to drift over the ridged edges of the mark branded into his flank.

He stalled her fingers and then brought them up to press a kiss against her knuckles.

"You don't have to hide anything from me, Raf," she said as she leaned back to stare at him somberly.

His throat thickened, but he forced himself to maintain eye contact. It was the least he could offer her, considering all the secrets he'd hidden from her for so long. "It's nothing."

"But what does it mean?" she asked, and a small frown notched twin lines between her golden brows. "How did you get it?"

He swallowed. "I don't want to talk about it."

"Why?"

"I don't like being reminded of the way I earned that brand."

"Earned?" Horror darkened her blue eyes, an innocent gaze that could never fathom the degradation of his past. "How could a child possibly earn such a thing?"

He simply stared at her, unwilling to sully their limited time together with the blackness of his shame.

Her eyes softened, glittering with an empathetic sheen of tears. "I hate that someone did such a horrific thing to you." She cupped his jaw and stared into his eyes before leaning forward to press a gentle kiss against his mouth. "I hate that someone scarred your beautiful soul."

He stilled, his limbs suddenly frozen and his lungs unable to draw breath.

She pushed upright and brushed the hair out of her eyes. "You don't believe me, do you?"

No words could navigate past his tight throat, so he remained miserably silent.

"You're beautiful, Rafael Chaves," she said as she dipped to brush her mouth over the taut skin of his chest. "Inside and out, you're the most beautiful man I know, and nothing you could have ever done would deserve such treatment."

When he still didn't answer, his chest cinched into a hard knot of denial, her hands joined in on her assertion. Inch by torturous inch, she worked to convince him while his body responded helplessly to her innocent devastation. Her fingers and mouth explored the heated skin stretched tight across his ribs, trailing heat and acceptance while he grappled for control.

"One of these days, you're going to believe me," she murmured as she moved even lower to press a warm kiss against his branded flesh. Her hand trailed west as she nuzzled the stark evidence of his wretched past, until she circled his hard length within her small, hot palm.

Despite his desire to remain strong, to keep the most debased part of himself separate and hidden, he felt his will weaken. He felt the anguished need to believe her, to forget all the reasons he wasn't good enough.

"One of these days," she promised and her fingers gently squeezed, driving him to the brink, "you're going to trust me and accept that I'm right."

Knowing she was wrong, but too selfish to prove it tonight, he reached for her. Her name escaped on a fractured breath as he rolled to his back, seized her hips and dragged her up to him. He silenced her beautiful, lying lips with his and drowned his tortured groan in her mouth. The sweet, wet forays of her tongue, coupled with her writhing against his stiffened flesh, made him ache with a desperate need to be inside her.

To forget.

To lose himself in pleasure while she gripped and clenched around him.

She came quietly, in soft, rolling pulls that drew out his own rapture while she arched and rocked atop him.

Wanting to prolong the moment, he forced himself to slow. To change the angle of his hips and the tempo of his fingers while he drew out her trembling release. When he could wait no longer, he drew her closer, closer, trying to communicate with hands and mouth and breath that he would never forget her.

That he loved her.

They made love twice more, until Sophia fell asleep in a damp, languorous heap. For a while, Rafael allowed himself to hold her, to steep himself in the pleasure of simply watching her. Dawn, despite his attempts to hold it at bay, hovered inexorably on the horizon, lightening the gray layer of fog that blanketed the city and bringing with it the miserable knowledge of what he could never have again. With excruciating, painful clarity, he knew he mustn't ever indulge in her sweetness again. His night with Sophia, a night of imagined pleasures that had haunted him for years, had fulfilled every fantasy he'd ever harbored. And now, it had come to an end.

For the few hours they'd been together, he'd shoved his conscience aside, determined to wring every moment of pleasure out of their forbidden tryst. He'd let himself kiss her, unwilling to resist the bowed arc of her upper lip, the sweet, slick heat of her small, scolding tongue. He'd allowed himself to touch every soft, scented inch of her, to finally, finally worship her the way he'd always longed. But it had been a mistake. A mistake he had to rectify before he brought devastation and ruin to the one person he'd vowed to protect.

Watching her sleep, so trusting and tousled, he felt a stab of guilt. He didn't want to hurt her. Ever. But what choice did he have now?

Cursing himself, he felt remorse tighten like a fist within his chest. If he'd just exercised a bit of restraint, she might have emerged from this night unscathed. They might have remained partners.

But no. He'd been weak. He'd succumbed. When he should have accepted the fiery flush of her outrage as his just due, he'd argued instead. He'd allowed his fear of losing her to overrule his good judgment and had joined her in that damned office. Even knowing how dangerous that small, private space could be, how reckless he'd been to follow her, touch her, kiss her, he hadn't stopped to think about the consequences. Reason had abandoned him, leaving him to operate on pure, carnal instinct.

And this time, there'd been no one to stop them. One taste of her mouth, and he'd been lost. Utterly, irrevocably lost. Caught in an avalanche of need so overwhelming, his common sense, his judgment and his promises to Turino and himself had ceased to matter. Nothing had mattered but Sophia and the desire that flared between them, a desire that had been smoldering for years. Like a match touched to flame, he'd been consumed with the need to possess her. To claim her, pleasure her and never come up for air.

It was a mistake that had nearly driven him to his knees, slamming into his gut with as much force as a fist. Now that he knew what being with Sophia was like, he couldn't trust himself around her anymore. He knew what it was like to watch her face as he pleasured her. He knew what it felt like to be deep, deep inside her when she pulsed around him. He knew, and the knowledge that he could never be with her again burned a hole in his chest. Things between them could never be the same again.

He had to leave. Permanently. Before he caused more damage than he already had.

But what if she's pregnant?

The thought brought a flush of warmth, a raw need to possess her, claim her and stand guard while her belly grew heavy with his child. It was barbaric, selfish and utterly, utterly wrong. He'd make a wretched father, would ruin whatever innocent life she brought into the world. He hadn't even been able to take care of his brother; he had no right to think he'd do better with a child of his own. Wanting to share a child with Sophia, craving a life and family he didn't deserve, would only bring devastation to them all.

Knowing he wanted it anyway shook him to the core.

Sick with self-loathing, he forced himself to abandon her, easing away from her soft, tousled warmth. She stirred, murmuring in her sleep and flinging a hand out to smack against his ribs. She slept the way she lived, sprawled in wild, unfettered abandon and with a slight smile on her face. She looked like she held a secret she couldn't wait to share, and he wanted to gather her up tight and never let her go. But he had no right. The golden-haired goddess with roseate skin and eyes the color of California sky deserved better.

Sophia awakened the morning after they'd made love, expecting to find Rafael's big, warm body stretched out next to her and his hot eyes touching her everywhere the lavender comforter didn't cover. With her heart light and her veins fuzzy with warmth, she'd reached for him only to discover an empty stretch of cold mattress and rumpled white sheets.

Two hours and several unreturned phone calls later, she finally realized he hadn't just ducked out for coffee and a paper, nor had he retreated to his own rooms for a quick shower and shave. He'd left, and a call to the front desk confirmed it. Two days before his scheduled flight home, he'd stolen away without a single word of farewell.

She eased her worries by telling herself that he couldn't have touched her the way he had, with his hands and lips and fingertips worshiping her in wordless praise, if he didn't feel *something* for her.

He was just running scared, she rationalized. Like always, she'd veered too close and he was backing away to regroup. She shouldn't take it personally.

She shouldn't blame him, or try to force him close when he wasn't ready. He'd fought the inevitable for as long as he'd known her, and she was willing to give him space to come to terms with the fact that their relationship had changed. She was willing to wait for him to finally admit that he loved her, and to forget all about those ridiculous lines he insisted on drawing between them.

Hadn't she been waiting for him for what seemed like a lifetime already? What was a few more days? she thought as she gathered her things to follow him home.

They were meant to be together. It was only a matter of time before he realized she was right.

So it was with an effervescent sense of anticipation that she returned to California, to the winery and partnership she now wanted more than life itself.

Sophia clung to her good mood and her hope for two interminable weeks before a dark doubt rose to eclipse her optimism. Two weeks! She hadn't seen or heard from him since their night in London, and her excuses for his lack of communication were wearing thin. Fear that she'd been wrong all along, that he'd viewed their night together as a colossal mistake and that she'd totally misinterpreted his feelings, plagued her with insecurity and worry.

She couldn't have been that off in her assessment of their relationship, could she?

Apparently, she could have.

And though she told herself he'd behaved just as she expected, it still hurt.

It had hurt even more the morning she'd learned she wasn't pregnant.

Fool that she was, she'd allowed herself to think things might be different than he'd said they would be. That a child might change things. That a child might make him admit the truth.

She'd allowed herself to hope, to dream about a future that would never be. She'd deluded herself into seeing things that weren't there, and convinced herself that the fantasy was real.

But with the truth staring her in the face, she could no longer deny it. Rafael hadn't just left London to regroup. He'd left *her.*

Too disheartened to dwell on his rejection, she threw herself into the business, actively following up on her London contacts and immersing herself in the day-to-day workings of a thriving winery. She learned more each day and fell exhausted into bed every night, praying for sleep to claim her thoughts and stem her tears.

It rarely did.

Four days later, Dolores returned early from her Thursday evening cleaning of Rafael's home. Sophia looked up from the books she'd been trying to balance, her back burning from fatigue and her eyes smarting from too many unshed tears. "Any word from Raf yet?"

Dolores lowered her purse to the table and didn't comment. Instead, she turned to empty the dish drainer with a quiet huff of irritation.

Silence was not Dolores's typical response, and Sophia studied the housekeeper's averted profile, wondering if she were hiding something. "What aren't you telling me?"

Dolores pressed her lips into a hard line of censure as she opened a cupboard and clanked a stack of plates inside. "Nothing. I'm just trying to gather my calm."

"Gather your calm?"

"Yes." The curt response came on the heels of a noisy sorting of flatware. "Because if I don't, I'm going to march back over there and slap that boy silly."

"Raf?" Sophia said, and her heart lurched into an uneven, galloping beat. "He's home?"

"Yes. He came home today, spewing a load of nonsense," Dolores said. "And he's meeting with a lawyer as we speak."

Sophia's hands froze around her pencil, and she was grateful for the way it concealed the trembling that claimed her limbs. "A lawyer? Why?"

Dolores's brows drew down into a dark scowl and she flung her hands up toward the ceiling. "Because he's a stubborn, idiot fool, that's why."

CHAPTER TWELVE

"I CAN'T believe you sent a lawyer to do your dirty work instead of talking to me yourself." Sophia strode into Rafael's black-and-grey office, her pale blue sleeveless dress and sandals a cool contrast to the fury in her distressed features.

"What dirty work?" It was the first time he'd seen her in nearly three weeks, and she was more beautiful than all of his aching memories combined.

"Don't play the innocent with me." She flung a stack of paperwork onto his desk and they scattered across the polished top, their fluorescent yellow "sign here" flags accusing him with their stark red arrows and blank signature lines. "Your lawyer just gave me those, and then had the temerity to imply that I should be pleased."

Rafael's gaze slid to the transfer of assets forms that his lawyer had just drawn up, and he felt the back of his scalp tighten. "Aren't you?"

"Do I look pleased?"

He straightened the papers without looking at her, arranging the pile while forcing steadiness to his hands. "I don't know why you wouldn't be. It's for the best."

"How is forfeiting your half of the business without consulting me first what's best?"

"I'm not forfeiting it," he said without any inflection at all.

"What do you call it, then?"

"Returning it to its rightful owner."

"It's *yours,* Raf."

"My job here is done." He ignored the way his lungs felt too tight to breathe. "I brought you home. I fulfilled my promise to your father. I'm not needed here any longer."

Her nostrils flared as she glared at him. "I've barely been here two months."

"You're a fast learner," he told her with a deliberate shrug. "And it's quite obvious you don't need me the way your father did."

"What?" she gasped. "Of course I do!"

He gestured toward the edge of his desk. "Why don't you grab that pen and we'll get these papers taken care of?"

"You've worked here for almost twenty years," she said after a quick glance at the pen. "Why would you throw it all away for no reason?"

"I'm not throwing it away. I'm giving it to you."

"I don't want it."

"You only think that right now. You're confused."

"I am *not* confused," she snapped. "I'm angry. And justifiably so. We're *partners.*"

"We can't be anymore, not after what happened in London. And once you've had some time to cool off, you'll see I'm right."

"How? You talk about my father's legacy and my responsibility to it, but you know this place will never survive without you here."

"It'll survive just fine. These past three weeks just proves it. You're smart, you learn quickly and wine-making is in your blood. The crew reports that you're doing better than any of us expected, and that your knack for blending rivals your father's. They all adore you, half of them are in love with you already, and with Manuel and Carlos as foremen, you won't need me at all."

"You're wrong." She placed her hands flat on his desk and leaned toward him, her blond hair sliding like a river of silk over one golden shoulder and arm. Her blue eyes were living flame, her distress bringing a flush to her cheeks and throat. "I don't agree to this. I won't. And you told me that neither of us can change our partnership without the other's agreement."

Resisting the urge to reach for her, he leaned back in his chair and laced his hands over his abdomen. Staring at the woman who might be pregnant with his child, at the woman he loved so much he could hardly breathe for wanting her, made his bones ache. "I lied."

"What?"

The dismissive shrug and false smile he offered her made his gut twist. He reminded himself that he deserved to lose her forever, that he deserved to lose *everything.* He never should have wanted what he couldn't have, and now he was paying the price. "I said whatever needed to be said to bring you home. I'd vowed to honor my promise to your father, and it didn't matter what lies I told to do it."

She jerked upright, her flushed skin assuming a paleness he hadn't seen since she thought she might be carrying his child. "So you're telling me the ends justify the means."

"Yes."

"And as long as Papa's little princess falls into line, as long as you fulfill your promise to him, integrity and trust don't matter."

He resisted the urge to recant his words, to tell her anything she wanted to hear if she'd just allow him to stay. "Yes."

Sophia searched his face for several long moments in silence, before confusion and hurt and doubt replaced her anger. "Why are you doing this?" she asked in a strangled voice. "You're better than this."

His entire body tensed, but he kept his expression aloof. He told himself that even if he could have stopped himself from hurting her, he wouldn't have. Driving her away, ripping his insides apart with one brutal yank, was the only way he could survive the pain of losing her. And even though he knew the pain in her eyes would haunt him for the rest of his life, he had no choice. It was for the best. She'd be better with him gone. "You never were a very good judge of character, were you?"

Her hand fluttered up to the neckline of her blue dress, pressing hard against her chest. She stepped back, her eyes wide and unblinking as hurt pulled at the corners of her mouth.

Dismissing her trust in such a cavalier fashion made it difficult to breathe. But if he didn't make her hate him, if he didn't make her glad that she was leaving, he'd change his mind. He'd beg her to let him love her and hold her and never let her go.

She seemed to regain her bearings enough to lift her chin and offer a tissue-thin smile. "I suppose it's never too late to learn from one's mistakes, is it?"

"No," he said, making himself sit there in arctic indifference despite the compulsion he felt to draw her close, comfort her and kiss the pain from her strained mouth. He forced his gaze to flick to her abdomen and back. "And speaking of mistakes, have you figured out whether you're pregnant or not?"

She went utterly still while her face blanched white.

"Well?"

She lifted her eyes to his, and he forced himself to stare directly into their clear depths despite the cost to his soul. "What if I were?" she asked in a choked voice. "Would it change anything?"

"Not really."

"So what do you care? If you're going to leave anyway, what does it matter?"

"I can certainly make sure my child never goes without. I can support you both in whatever way you deem necessary."

"Don't worry," she blurted. "I won't burden you with another Turino you don't want," she said. The pained timbre of her words lanced his lungs like the lash of a whip.

"I won't shirk my responsibilities," he said in a cool, calm voice of reason. "If you're pregnant, I want to know about it."

"Of course you do," she said, her hurt lending a sharp edge to her voice. "You've never been anything but a bastion of responsibility and obligation, have you?"

He pressed his mouth into a firm line and remained silent, his past and Paolo's death clear evidence to the contrary.

"No one likes to feel like an obligation," she continued. "I should know. And for the record, I'd never allow our child to know you viewed him as a penance you had to pay. If you're incapable of loving him and raising him as his father, then we'd be better off without you or your *support.*"

His jaw flexed while his stomach muscles drew tight with dread. And anticipation. And hope. "Are you saying what I think you're saying?"

"No." Her eyes were shiny with unshed tears and her

mouth trembled despite her visible efforts to look composed. "I was only speaking hypothetically."

"Hypothetically?"

"I'm not pregnant," she clarified.

Disappointment wrenched hard within his lungs, but he forced the lie out anyway. "I'm glad to hear it."

She stared at him for a moment without speaking, her wide blue eyes filled with confused pain. "I'm not," she finally confessed.

The words hit him like a fist, driving the air from his lungs. "What?"

Her small hand pressed against her abdomen and her breath came in fragmented, shallow pulls. "Crazy, isn't it? I wanted to be pregnant. Whether you would have welcomed the news or not, I wanted your child. To have a part of you that would love me and not reject me."

He swallowed thickly, unable to frame a suitable reply.

"But these past three weeks have proven to me that it's not to be. *We're* not to be."

I'm sorry. "No."

"I realize that now." She inhaled sharply, bracing her shoulders as she shook off her sadness. "I know the truth about how you feel and I accept it. You won't ever love me and even thought it hurts, I've come to terms with it. So if you're leaving because you think I'm going to demand more than you want to give, don't."

Hearing her absolve him of the consequences of their lovemaking made the knife of guilt twist sharply in his gut. "Soph—"

"Don't." She held up a palm, her body taut and her mouth trembling. "You don't have to explain. I know making love to me was a mistake. That it didn't mean anything to you."

He contemplated her words in miserable silence, wanting to tell her it had meant *everything* to him.

"I just want you to understand that things here don't have to change just because we spent one night together." She firmed her chin, reminding him of how she'd always rallied after being hurt as a child. "It doesn't have to derail your life and ruin everything we could build as partners here."

He dragged his focus away from her sweet face and then pushed to a stand, moving to stare sightlessly out of the bank of black north windows.

"I promise I won't ask for anything more than you're willing to give. Not ever again." She inhaled again and then followed him. She stepped close enough to stand at his side, their reflections eerily transparent in the waning light. "There's no reason we can't make this work," she said. "We can redraw those lines you insist on having, and pretend London never happened."

He stiffened at her nearness, his skin on fire where her heat warmed him, and stepped away from her with a shake of his head. "No."

"Why not?" she insisted. "If I can move past it, why can't you?"

Their eyes met in their reflection for several long moments, the silence stretching between them like a living thing.

"I swear we can pretend London never happened," she urged as she turned to face him, pressing him to tell her their night together had meant nothing to him. That *she* meant nothing to him.

He met her gaze, the desire to touch her so strong he could taste it on his tongue. "No. Even if I wanted to, I couldn't. London happened and there's no going back."

She stood beside him in silence, the weight of her stare multiplying his guilt tenfold.

"I can't forget that night or what I did to you," he growled. "Ever." He swallowed as he dropped his gaze to his knotted hands and firmed his mouth. "Which is why I have to leave. No matter what we do, that night will always be between us."

"So what if it is?" she asked softly, her small fingers fluttering up to rest on his rigid shoulder. "We can just chalk it up as yet another of my impulsive decisions, a choice I should never have made."

"It wasn't just your choice." He shrugged off her touch and moved away from her, placing distance between them before he trusted himself to meet her eyes. "It was mine. And I can't ever undo it." *Nor can I promise I won't try to repeat it.*

"Am I asking you to?"

Her quiet response, the acceptance she always, always offered, made him want to haul her close, bury his head against her breast and beg her to forgive him when he deserved nothing but her disgust. "You don't have to. I'm leaving regardless."

Again, slim fingers reached for his arm. "Would you still leave if Papa were here?"

The dual betrayal of Turino and Sophia sat in his gut like twin boulders, growing heavier with each passing day. "If your father knew what happened in London, the things I did to you, he'd banish me himself." His left eye twitched and his mouth tightened before he continued. "But even if he didn't, Turino would welcome the additional property I'm leaving to his estate. With what I'm adding to your holdings, Turino's legacy will live on for generations to come."

"Generations?" A small huff of laughter accompanied

the word. "And just who, exactly, is going to father these generations of Turinos?"

He dragged his arm from beneath her fingers, unable to remain immobile while she hovered so close, touching him. "I'm sure you'll find someone," he told her as he retreated to his desk, using the large piece of furniture as a barricade to shore up against his weakness for her.

"Like who?" she asked. "Alexander?"

A dark and bleak anger accompanied the name, but Rafael swallowed it back. "If he makes you happy, then yes."

"He wanted to follow me here, you know," she said from where he'd left her. "He wanted to start a relationship with me and confessed his love for me."

His hands curled into fists against the desktop while the air in his lungs refused to move.

A morose half smile pulled at her mouth. "And the ironic part of it is, he wanted to follow me so I'd be off-limits to you." A shake of her head accompanied the admission. "As if you'd need additional reasons to stay away from me."

He remained silent while his heartbeat thundered in his ears.

"And you know what?" she asked. "I *should* be with him. I admire him. He's handsome. He's generous and kind. He's one of my best friends and I know he'd never, ever hurt me."

"Then why didn't you invite him to join you?"

"Did you want me to?" she asked as she lifted her gaze to his.

I don't want you with anyone but me. As difficult as it was, he forced his face to remain expressionless as he formed the words. "I want you to be happy."

She stood without moving, staring at him while color gathered in her cheeks. "Do you, Raf? Do you really?"

"Of course I do."

Tears brightened her eyes, but she battled them back before they fell. "And you think Alexander will make me happy."

He has to. "Yes."

She blinked twice while her mouth wobbled. "You're right. He's a wonderful man. And what woman wouldn't be happy with a good man who loved her?"

"Soph—"

"Except I can't love him back," she confessed in a brittle, cracking voice. "I've tried, but my stupid heart won't listen."

Palpable relief, relief he knew he had no business feeling, flooded his chest.

"Do you want to know why?"

No. Yes. Tell me.

"I can't love him because I seem to be incapable of loving anyone but you." A wet, miserable bubble of laughter clogged in her throat. "How pathetic is that?"

His chest tightened to the point of pain. Remaining where he stood while she fought her tears required a strength he hadn't realized he possessed.

After what felt like an eternity of silence, she finally hauled in a shuddering breath and pressed the back of her wrist to her mouth before straightening with a bright, if strained, smile. "Right." She smoothed her hair back with her free hand and then reached for the pen on his desk. "I said I wouldn't ask for anything beyond partnership, and here I've already broken my word. My apologies." She took the pen and bent to lift the stack of papers. "I'll sign these at home if you don't mind, because if I stay here,

I'm liable to make an even bigger fool of myself and beg you to change your mind."

Later, after he'd watched her until she disappeared into the night's cold embrace, he closed his blinds and tried to lose himself in a bottle of Scotch. Halfway through, with his fingers too clumsy to pour another shot and his lips and tongue too numb to taste the burn, Rafael realized no amount of alcohol could blur the clarity of his memories.

He still saw Sophia in every shaft of moonlight and behind his eyes whenever he blinked. He still smelled the faint fragrance of her perfume on his hands, still tasted the heady sweetness of her mouth beneath his. No matter how hard he tried to forget, he couldn't rid his mind of its memories. Sophia haunted him, just as she always had.

Around 9:00 a.m. the next morning, after he'd packed his office into haphazard stacks of boxes and then slumped into a dreamless, drunken sleep over his empty desk, he awoke with a headache the size of a wine cask. The bright shafts of sunlight Dolores had invited into his office didn't help, either.

He shot a glare at Dolores and lifted a hand to block the light, trying to minimize the stabbing pain behind his right eye. "Get the hell out of here," he told the interfering housekeeper.

She ignored him, opening even more blinds with efficient twists of her wrists. "What on Earth did you say to Sophia yesterday? I've never seen her so quiet and sad."

"Let any more light in here, and you're fired," he groused.

"You know Sophia will just hire me back," she said before she cranked the final blinding light into spotlight precision against his face. "You need to apologize to that poor girl, and you need to do it now."

"Stay out of it," he groaned.

"Not a chance," she scolded. "You two are the closest thing I've got to a family. And now that you're home, I refuse to stand by while you make her miserable."

"She'll get over it." Rafael stood and the floor tilted dangerously up to meet him until he steadied himself against the edge of his desk. "For God's sake, shut the damn blinds."

"What is wrong with you?" Dolores asked, completely ignoring his edict. "Sophia's the best thing that ever happened to you. Why would you want to deliberately hurt her?"

"I don't have to answer to you."

"Well, you need to answer to *someone* before you ruin two lives for no good reason," she huffed.

"I'm not ruining her life." He glared at her, or at least at the fuzzy outline that had Dolores's shape. "I'm saving it."

She moved closer, stabbing a finger into his chest. "I'd never thought it possible, but you are more of a bullheaded fool than Turino ever was."

Rafael dropped his head, closing his eyes against the lurching sensation in his gut. "I'm only doing what I think is best."

"How can rejecting the girl you love, the girl you've loved for as long as I've known you, be what's best?"

Rafael swallowed. Hard. And then raised his blurry eyes to Dolores's disappointed brown ones. "Trust me. It is."

Dolores shook her head, her network of frown lines softening into pity. "She loves you, Raf."

He hated that his hands shook at that. "She deserves someone better."

"Oh, Raf." She lifted one chapped hand and cupped his

cheek. "What's it going to take for you to believe that you deserve better, too?"

He merely stared at her in wretched silence.

She studied his eyes for another long moment before she dropped her hand and sighed. "I hope you realize how wrong you are before it's too late."

CHAPTER THIRTEEN

AFTER Dolores left, Rafael dragged himself up to his bed and slept until nightfall. He awoke disoriented and angry at the world and with his head feeling like it had been stuffed with briars. His brain hurt, his eyes hurt and his body felt as if he'd been run over by a truck. He showered, brushed his teeth and changed into clean clothes, but nothing helped.

He doubted anything ever could.

So he wandered his big empty house until restlessness drove him outside into the soft darkness that cloaked his vineyard and layered his porch in shades of black and plum. The evening breeze cooled his heated skin, bringing with it the scent of soil and grapes and night. Too miserable to appreciate any of it, Rafael stood at the edge of his whitewashed steps and glowered out at the shadowed land he'd sown with his own hands.

He needed to clear his thoughts of Sophia, to remind himself of all the reasons she deserved someone better. He needed to remember all the reasons she could never be happy with him.

She didn't even know him. She thought she did, but she didn't. He'd never allowed her to see the Rafael that crouched beneath the thin veneer of civilization he'd donned. He'd never shown her the man capable of hurting those he loved most. The man capable of violence. Of death.

He stepped off the wooden porch and tried to lose himself in the night, walking the darkened rows of vines until his shoulders bowed with fatigue, until the sliver of moon that hung overhead had begun its descent to the horizon.

Hating how he was always, always drawn to the one woman he couldn't have, he cast an angry glare at the shadowed outbuildings of Sophia's property. A faint light leaking from one of the Turino Winery's windows made him go ominously still.

Rafael's skin prickled. Who could be in the winery at this hour?

It took him two minutes to sprint to the building's unlocked door, and another minute for his breathing to calm while he eased the door open. His eyes adjusted to the shadowed silhouettes of stainless steel and wood within the main level as he inched his way inside. The large interior was dark, but the pale light that had drawn his attention rimmed the closed door that led to Turino's cellars.

His crew knew better than to leave the lights on overnight. None of them would have been so careless. Rafael held his breath and crept closer, cocking his head as he listened. A strange sound filtered from below, a jerky, choked snuffling he didn't recognize.

He tensed, his hands balling into fists while his heart raced beneath his ribs. "Who's there?" he called.

An abrupt silence met his query.

Jerking the door open, he yelled into the musty space below. "Show yourself," he demanded, "or I'll have you arrested for trespassing!"

When no culprit was forthcoming, he thundered down the wooden steps, his boots clanking loudly as he sprang to the floor and landed with his knees cocked and his fists raised.

Only to discover Sophia. Alone. And crying.

Sophia had lurched to her feet, her body silhouetted in the faint light as she flattened herself against a row of oaken barrels. Blotchy-faced and terrified, she didn't relax her defensive stance until he straightened and lowered his hands.

"What are you doing down here?" he asked, though he needn't have bothered. It was obvious she was weeping… privately. Her beautiful blue eyes were swollen and her cheeks were damp with tears.

"What are *you* doing down here?" she shot back, jutting her chin up.

"I saw the light. It's never on at night and I…" He exhaled and ran a palm over his mouth, disturbed by the evidence of tears on her face and neck. She looked uncharacteristically dismal, his strong Sophia undone by pain. Pain he'd caused. She wore the same white T-shirt and gray shorts she'd worn the first night he'd seen her, and the neckline of her shirt was damp and stuck to her skin. Her hair was a mess and he felt so unmanned by her tears, he was momentarily at a loss for words.

"Well, it's just me, so there's no need to concern yourself," she told him tightly.

"You're crying."

"So you'll understand my desire for privacy." Her nose was stuffed up, making her voice sound plugged and nasally.

The fact that she wept stunned him. In all the years he'd known Sophia, he'd never seen her succumb to tears. Ever. She was not a woman easily dismantled, and he was not a man to be affected by feminine tears. But his pulse was quaking and he couldn't seem to drawn a decent breath.

"Go away," she demanded.

"No."

"I don't want you here!"

He watched her helplessly, refusing her request. "I know."

She glared at him mutinously, pressing her mouth into a tight, wounded seam while her eyes filled anew. Soon, her shoulders began to quiver beneath withheld sobs and her desperate attempts to stem the tide of sorrow failed. When it appeared she could contain her tears no longer, she spun to present her back and dropped her face into her hands.

Rafael stared at her T-shirt, stretched across her narrow shoulder blades, at the haphazard ponytail of gold, and the escaped strands that curled at her nape. He fought the urge to haul her into his arms, to turn her against his body while she wept into his chest.

Instead, he said, "I hate seeing you this way."

"Then leave!"

It felt like his lungs were caught in a vise. "I can't."

"Just go already!" she wailed into her hands. "I don't want you here!"

He remained, disarmed, unable to abandon her while she was so distressed. Especially when he knew her hurt feelings were his fault. After a few moments, she sank to her knees and rocked forward, her silent sobs so wracking, her ribs shook. His own chest tightened and he felt a hard knot thicken his throat. Swallowing against it didn't seem to help, and when he could bear it no longer, he dropped to a squat and reached for her bowed shoulders. "Soph," he murmured in a low voice, "come here."

A fervent shake of her head denied him. "Just l-leave," she said through her fingers. "G-go away."

"No." He couldn't make his fingers abandon the soft

slope of her nape, couldn't release the tenuous hold on his own remorse. Tugging on her until she rotated toward him, he lifted both palms to the sides of her neck. "I'm not leaving until I know you're okay."

"Don't lie to me!" She lifted devastated eyes to his. "Because you *are* leaving and I won't be okay. Ever. Being nice to me now just makes it worse!"

Emotion slammed through him and it took supreme effort to keep from pulling her close. "I'm sorry," he said quietly. "But it's for the best. And it'll get better with time. I promise."

Tears swelled and spilled again, tracking down her cheeks in wet, miserable streaks. "How?" she insisted in a choked voice. "I d-don't know h-how to do this by m-myself," came her choppy explanation, interspersed with sobs. "And I d-don't even…even—" Sophia clamped her mouth shut as she battled a fresh surge of emotion. "I don't even want to t-try without you here. I thought I was s-stronger now, that I could b-be your p-partner and not want m-more—" She waged a valiant fight against an onslaught of new tears, lifting brimming eyes to the ceiling and inhaling noisily before she struggled to continue. "But I was w-wrong…I knew it before I even c-came h-here. I should have n-never left L-London." She blinked furiously, but her efforts to stem the fresh tide of tears did little to contain them.

Kneeling before her, Rafael watched helplessly as she bowed over her hands again, weeping until her entire body shook. He couldn't breathe while he watched her struggle for control, his heart quaking along with her quivering shoulders. *Don't cry, Soph...I can't bear it.*

But she cried anyway, holding the sobs back with white-tipped fingers until they leaked through in pitiful, choked mewls of grief. Pressure built within his own chest until he could no longer fight the need to hold her.

"Soph…it's my fault…hush…you'll be fine…I promise…" Still on his knees before her, he pulled her into his arms and she offered no resistance, sliding limply into him as he tenderly tucked her head against his chest.

"Oh, Raaaf…" she sobbed jerkily as he drew her into his lap and settled to the cool concrete floor with his back against the stacked row of oak barrels. "Why does l-life have to be so h-hard?" She burrowed against him, her hands gripping his shirt as she wept against his chest.

"Shh…it'll be okay," he soothed as he cupped the back of her head and pressed her face against his throat. He held her within the circle of his arms while her tears dampened his shirt and skin, wishing he could somehow make up for his callousness. But he couldn't. He was a brute, incapable of framing suitable words of solace. So he simply held her, in silence, until her sobs faded to soft hiccups, her arm looped weakly about his neck.

Dipping his cheek to the top of her head, he waited until she slowly grew quiet and her breath evened. There were no words he could offer to ease her pain, no combination of syllables that could communicate the consolation he wished to give her.

"I hate that you're seeing me like this," she eventually offered in a low, muffled voice.

"Considering the state I was in when your father found me," he chided, "I'd say we're even."

She sighed shakily, and he felt her breasts move against his chest. She scrubbed her face against his chest and mumbled into his skin. "No, we're not. You were beautiful even then. Bruised, bleeding and angry at the world, you were still the most beautiful thing I'd seen."

"A monster isn't beautiful," he corrected, unwilling to

leave her vulnerable without offering some small sliver of his own weakness up for her inspection. "Not when I earned each one of those bruises and deserved every bit of their pain."

She grew still within his arms, suspended in silence while she absorbed his confession. "How can you say such awful things about yourself?" she finally asked.

He didn't answer for a moment, steeping himself in the bittersweet pleasure of holding her one final time. Because he knew once he told her, once she knew the truth, she'd turn from him in disgust. How could she not?

So he remained as he was, pressed close to the woman he loved as he weighed the words that would separate them forever. His lips rested against the crooked part of her hair, his hand idly trailing from nape to waist and back again until he finally offered, "My brother died the day your father found me."

"Your brother?" she repeated, pressing back enough that she could meet his eyes. "I didn't know you had a brother."

He pressed his mouth into a tight line, his throat suddenly tight with emotion. "His name was Paolo. And he was nine years old."

Sympathy softened her expression as she studied his face. "What happened?"

Bleak devastation rose within his chest and he averted his eyes so she couldn't read the blackness he hid within.

"Tell me," she urged, her gentle hand rising to cup his jaw and turning him back to her.

Swallowing thickly, he forced himself to continue. "Remember when you asked me about the mark on my hip?"

"Yes," she whispered as her breath stilled.

"The man who branded me, who branded *us*...he wasn't a good man."

She said nothing, simply waiting for him to continue.

"He branded both Paolo and me—" his fists clenched involuntarily at the memory of his brother's cries "—so we'd never forget that we belonged to him."

"Oh, Raf," she breathed while her face blanched white. "I'm so sorry."

"It's not your fault," he insisted. "It was mine."

Her eyes, filled with transparent compassion, searched his. "How could such a thing possibly have been your fault?"

As difficult as it was, he steeled himself against her sympathy and forced the damning truth past his throat. "If I'd been better…if I'd been good, our mother wouldn't have sold us to him."

Horror, tinged with outrage, brought the color back to her cheeks. "Your mother *sold* you?"

"She had no choice," he insisted. "I was a violent, rebellious bastard who scared the life out of a woman too frail to defend herself."

"Against a child?"

"She knew I lived to hate, and that I carried a rage too terrifying to control."

Her brows knitted in misplaced fury while her hand slid down to the bunched muscles of his shoulder. "With a mother like that, I'd think you had good reason to be angry."

"No," he confessed mercilessly, wanting her to understand the truth about him, to stop her blind defense of his character when he possessed none to defend. "She sold me to someone vicious enough to direct my talents while keeping me under a tight rein."

"I don't believe it," she said, gripping his shoulder instead of recoiling as she should. "That woman was selfish and weak and wrong. And if I knew how to find her, I'd wring her neck myself for doing such a beastly, unforgivable thing to her own child."

"I deserved it."

Shaking her head while her mouth firmed in rebuttal, she jostled him with her narrow hand. "No, Raf. No child deserves to suffer such atrocities. I don't care what he does."

"Even if he kills his brother?"

She stared at him in silence for several seconds before she shook her head again. "I don't believe it. There's no way you could have killed your brother."

"I may as well have," he choked out. "When I should have protected him, I didn't. And he died."

"I'm sure you had no choice in the matter."

"I did. I did have a choice." He clenched his jaw against the debilitating flash of pain the memory wrought. "And Paolo died because I made the wrong one."

"And what choice was that, Raf?" she demanded while her free hand lifted to tip his chin. "To survive?"

"To leave," he answered as he lifted his head from her fingers. "When I should have stayed to protect him, I left."

"I'm sure you would have stayed if you could have." Her gentle hands returned to his face, denying him his retreat as they tracked faint, soothing caresses along the tense lines of cheek and jaw. "You'd never willingly allow harm to come to someone you loved," she told him. "If there's one thing I know about you, it's that."

The statement was so patently untrue that Rafael almost laughed. If he weren't so wretchedly miserable, he probably would have. As it was, the breath merely huffed in his chest while he stared helplessly at Sophia. "Until your father brought me here," he confessed mercilessly, "I was a thug. A criminal. I lived to steal, to scavenge and hide and hurt strangers who'd done me no harm at all. I was incapable of goodness." Seeing Sophia's clear blue eyes fill with sympathy made his throat tighten. "Don't look at me like that," he said hoarsely.

"Like what?" she asked.

"Like I'm worthy of saving."

"You are."

He inhaled sharply through his nose. The forgiveness and acceptance he read in her eyes eroded his control, threatening to undo him altogether. But he couldn't be weak. Not again. "I'm not."

She clucked softly, concern notching faint lines between her brows. "Of course you are."

He shook his head against her palm, her misplaced faith in him making his gut twist in painful denial.

Both hands cupped his face, stilling his denial. "You're the best man I know, Rafael Chaves. And anyone who thinks otherwise doesn't deserve to know you."

"The only decent thing in my life was Paolo. And I…I let him die when I should have been there to help him." He swallowed and then forced himself to continue.

Her hands slid to his nape and she jostled him gently. "It's not your fault. You were a child."

Unwilling to hide behind her unfounded excuses, he plowed forward. She deserved to know the soulless thief who'd taken her with such clumsy, desperate abandon. He owed her the truth. And even though he knew she'd never look at him the same way again, he forced the words past his closing throat.

"I wasn't," he insisted. "I was fifteen. A selfish brute more interested in his next mark than in the welfare of his brother."

"You were a boy who'd never known love. Or softness. Or caring. A boy doing his best to survive."

Appalled by the blinding desire to lose himself in her

acceptance, to halt his reckless confession so she'd keep loving him, he forced the wretched, unvarnished truth past his lips. He spewed out all the horrific details of his depraved existence, telling her of the crimes he'd committed and the beatings he'd endured, the cage he'd slept in, the rotten scraps he'd been forced to consume when his daily take had been too low. He told her of all the humiliations he'd withstood, and how each degradation had brought new layers of darkness to his soul. He told her he was an animal, a minion of a demon who'd allowed his little brother to die a brutal, painful death.

"And what about Paolo?" she murmured softly, her hand still gentle against his rigid neck. "Was little Paolo a minion as well?"

"No," he choked out. "He wasn't. He didn't deserve anything that monster did to him."

"While you did?" she gently admonished. "How does that make sense?"

"It does," he persisted, lifting his hands between them. "I didn't just allow Paolo to die. I murdered a man. With my bare hands."

"I'm sure you were simply protecting yourself and a brother you loved."

"No. Paolo was already dead. I wanted revenge," he insisted, his tone pitched low with self-loathing. "I fought that *diablo* until he fell, until his face was a bloody mess and my knuckles were split down to the bone. I can still hear the sound as he hit the floor, can still feel the rush of victory when he didn't rise again. I watched him die, and I didn't care. I was glad. Glad. So I'm no better than that monster, and yet I dare to touch you, to act as if I'm worthy of even one—"

"Hush," she interrupted. Both her hands lifted to mold around his rough fingers and she waited until he met her eyes. "You are worthy, Raf. Of everything you could possibly wish to claim."

"I'm not." Anguish shredded his tone. "I can't be. I have no conscience, no honor, and beneath this civilized veneer I hide behind, I have no soul. You're the only reason I've even tried to pretend otherwise."

"You're wrong." Her face, angelic in its compassion, showed no evidence that she'd even heard all the horrible things he'd divulged. "The fact that you survived so many atrocities despite the world's efforts to kill everything that is good in you speaks to your resilience and your strength of character. You have a core of goodness that can't be destroyed, Raf, a rare, beautiful soul, and I won't accept you maligning it."

"You didn't listen to me," he insisted. "If you heard anything I said, you'd know I—"

"I did hear. I just choose to interpret the evidence differently than you." She brought the tips of his fingers to her lips and then lowered their joined hands to her chest. "You survived a childhood that should have destroyed you. You emerged strong, honorable and brave. And I love you even more, now that I know."

"You can't," he said thickly. "You deserve much better."

"Why don't you let me be the judge of what I deserve?" she declared as her hands tightened about his.

When he didn't answer, she leaned to wrap her arms around his tense shoulders. They were quiet for a long time, her face pressed against his neck while his pulse beat unsteadily beneath her warm weight. "Do you know I loved you from that very first day?" she eventually asked. "Wild, wounded and angry boy that you were, I recognized the goodness in you. I wanted to absorb your pain and make you smile. I wanted to make you happy. Did you know that?"

He closed his eyes and nodded against her soft hair. She smelled like she'd always smelled, a sweet, heady combination of innocence and stubbornness and courage. He wanted to lay her down and worship her until the past disappeared and the future spread out before them, clean and bright and new.

"I knew you wanted to scare me away," she said. "But I also knew you would never hurt me, so I kept trying no matter how many times you snapped at me." Her fingertips traced small circles over his back, until sensitive shivers chased down his spine.

A forlorn smile brought a sting of regret that he'd treated her so poorly. "You always were too trusting."

"While you didn't realize I thrived on the challenge of taming you until it was too late, did you? Poor, wounded man, you never learned how to fight against love."

Unwilling to resist any longer, he allowed himself to embrace her, to wrap her softness within his arms. "You're right," he answered in a low, muffled voice. "But it wasn't from lack of trying."

"Are you still going to push me away now?" she asked.

He hauled in a deep breath. "I should, but I can't. Even though I don't want to hurt you, you're the only good thing in my life and I can't bear the thought of losing you."

She leaned back to look into his eyes. "You don't have to, Raf. Ever. You're part of me and I'm not going anywhere."

"Did you know I thought you were an angel that first day? I woke up and saw you and thought I'd somehow ended up in heaven. And it didn't make any sense, because I'd expected hell."

"Is that why you snarled at me?"

"I snarled at you because what I felt for you scared me. I didn't want to hurt you. I didn't want to ruin your innocence or pollute you in any way." He stroked a palm down her warm back, pressing her again to his chest. "I told myself every day to stay away from you, but I couldn't do it. I craved you like the earth craves the sun. I lived for the time we were together, for the sweet torture of your nearness. And even though I know I can't ever deserve you, I can't let you go."

She tipped her head back to gaze wetly up at him. "Then don't."

"I'm sorry I hurt you," he said as he traced a finger over her swollen eyelid and blotchy brow. "And I'm sorry I made you cry."

"You're forgiven," she said with a soft, trembling smile.

"I love you, Sophia." His chest hurt with the confession he'd held inside for so long. "So much so, I don't know how to contain it all."

"Then don't," she whispered, leaning forward to brush her lips against his. "Just love me and trust that I want everything you have to give."

He kissed her then, tasting her mouth and her sweetness and her forgiveness, and wondered how he'd ever thought he could live without her. She made him whole. She healed him. And he wanted to spend the rest of his life with her. Loving her.

"I dreamed of this, you know," she said as she angled back to touch her fingertips to his mouth. Her eyes were wet again and she looked so beautiful it made his throat hurt. "Every day and every night for as long as I can remember, I've dreamed of you telling me you loved me." A rueful smile caught at her mouth as her gaze slid down to her wrinkled T-shirt. "Except in my dreams, we weren't in a cellar and I was dressed in something a little more romantic."

"I love you no matter what you wear," he told her as he brushed his thumb beneath her eye.

Her eyes spilled over and she sniffed through her smile. "Say it again."

"Marry me," he said instead.

"Marry you?" she repeated while sunlight dawned in her blue eyes.

"Yes. I want you to be the last thing I see each night and the first thing I see each morning. Always. I want to kiss you and hold you and make love to you and watch you when you sleep. I want to make you breakfast in bed, rub your feet when you're tired and marvel as your belly grows heavy with my children. And I know I don't deserve you and I know I'll probably—"

"Children?" she interrupted breathlessly.

"Or not," he amended hastily. "I want whatever will make you happy."

"*You* make me happy." She reached to wrap her arms around his neck and tipped her head back to stare up at him. "Deliriously, gloriously happy. So yes, Rafael Chaves, I will marry you."

Relief flooded his chest and he bent to press a kiss against her upturned mouth.

She pulled back with a smug smile and then burrowed against his chest. "But only if we name the first of our many sons after Papa. He's the one who brought us back together, you know."

A surge of gratitude toward the man who'd saved him and brought Sophia into his life made Rafael's throat thicken. "He did, didn't he?"

She murmured her agreement and cuddled even closer. "I think he'd be quite pleased with how his little scheme worked out. His favorite surrogate son, his wayward daughter and his winery, all together and making plans for babies. What could make him prouder?"

He couldn't seem to stop the wellspring of joy that rushed through him at her words. The scent of her skin, the feel of her pressed against his chest, filled him with a happiness he'd thought permanently out of reach. Dipping his forehead to hers, he stared at her until the darkness of his past disappeared in the sunny depths of her eyes.

"I want to make love to you," he told her in a ragged whisper.

"Here?" she asked him with a coy smile.

"Everywhere."

EPILOGUE

A MERE ten months later, Sophia and Rafael lay facing each other on her narrow hospital bed, their beautiful son nestled between them. A pastel cap of blue and green covered a startling amount of black hair, curled fists lay temporarily still alongside perfect ears and a miniature mouth worked in silent sucking motions.

He was perfect.

"He has your brows," Sophia observed before running a single fingertip down their child's downy cheek to the center of his tiny chin. "And Papa's stubborn jaw."

When Rafael didn't answer, Sophia lifted her gaze to find her husband staring at her, his heart in his eyes. "Do you know how amazing you are?"

"I couldn't have done it without you," she whispered as happiness filled her heart to brimming. Though there'd been a few moments when the nurses had been more concerned for Rafael than for her pending delivery, he'd rallied. She'd needed him, and he'd been there every step of the way. He'd fed her ice chips, rubbed her back and counted through her contractions when it felt like they'd never end.

"You'll never have to," he said. "Not as long as I live."

"I know." When she'd discovered she was pregnant, she'd fretted that he'd revert to his overbearing, protective role, and that he'd hobble her with a confinement wrought by fear. But he'd been amazingly calm. It was if unburdening himself of his past, of his guilt and pain, had left him more willing to fully engage in the present and trust in the future.

Each time he'd touched her, his warm hands possessive and gentle against her swelling belly, she'd felt their connection strengthen and his faith in their future grow. Sharing the miracle of their baby's first kick, walking hand in hand through their thriving vineyard while autumn transformed into winter and then spring, they'd learned to embrace the second chance at happiness that life had provided them.

And as impossible as it seemed, it felt that her love for Rafael grew with each passing day. Joy permeated their interactions and underscored their days. It was as if the walls Rafael had built between them had ceased to exist, replaced by love and hope and trust.

She still had to pinch herself at times, just to ensure that it was real. That the life they'd built together was more than just a dream.

Against all odds, they were happy. Complete. She'd become less impulsive and more grounded. Rafael's serious intensity had softened and an irrepressible lightness had replaced the edge of anger that had dominated his interactions for so long. He laughed now, teased and joked and smiled. The crew, who'd always respected him, truly loved him with an adoration that bordered on worship. He'd become the touchstone for them all, and rather than being weighed down by the responsibility, he'd thrived.

They all had.

Sophia smiled into her husband's eyes and reached to cup his whisker-roughened face. Unwilling to leave her alone once her contractions had begun, Rafael hadn't been home or slept for over twenty-four hours. But even with fatigue drawing shadows beneath his eyes, he looked content. Exhausted, but content. "I've been thinking about what we'll name him," she told Rafael.

He cocked his head drowsily, a proud smile curving his mouth as he shifted his focus to their slumbering infant. Rafael's big, brown hand curved possessively over their son's capped head, his thumb tracing the knitted edge of blue while his throat worked with his swallow. "Dante?"

"For Papa, yes." She dropped her hand atop Rafael's and waited until his eyes returned to her. "But I thought we could name him for Paolo, too. Paolo Dante Chaves."

Rafael stared at her without speaking for a moment, his dark eyes turning suspiciously bright. "I think he'd have liked that."

She smiled at him through a sheen of tears. "I'm glad."

"I love you, Sophia Chaves," he said in a voice gone rough with emotion.

Her tears spilled over, whether from hormones or a happiness that was too big to hold inside, she couldn't tell. "I love you, too."

Then he leaned over their sleeping child and kissed her tears away.

* * * * *

Read on for a sneak preview of Carol Marinelli's
PUTTING ALICE BACK TOGETHER!

Hugh hired bikes!

You know that saying: 'It's like riding a bike, you never forget'?

I'd never learnt in the first place.

I never got past training wheels.

'You've got limited upper-body strength?' He stopped and looked at me.

I had been explaining to him as I wobbled along and tried to stay up that I really had no centre of balance. I mean *really* had no centre of balance. And when we decided, fairly quickly, that a bike ride along the Yarra perhaps, after all, wasn't the best activity (he'd kept insisting I'd be fine once I was on, that you never forget), I threw in too my other disability. I told him about my limited upper-body strength, just in case he took me to an indoor rock-climbing centre next. I'd honestly forgotten he was a doctor, and he seemed worried, like I'd had a mini-stroke in the past or had mild cerebral palsy or something.

'God, Alice, I'm sorry—you should have said. What happened?'

And then I had had to tell him that it was a self-diagnosis. 'Well, I could never get up the ropes at the gym at school.' We were pushing our bikes back. 'I can't blow-dry the back of my hair…' He started laughing.

Not like Lisa who was laughing at me—he was just laughing and so was I. We got a full refund because we'd only been on our bikes ten minutes, but I hadn't failed. If anything, we were getting on better.

And better.

We went to St Kilda to the lovely bitty shops and I found these miniature Russian dolls. They were tiny, made of tin or something, the biggest no bigger than my thumbnail. Every time we opened them, there was another tiny one, and then another, all reds and yellows and greens.

They were divine.

We were facing each other, looking down at the palm of my hand, and our heads touched.

If I put my hand up now, I can feel where our heads touched.

I remember that moment.

I remember it a lot.

Our heads connected for a second and it was alchemic; it was as if our minds kissed hello.

I just have to touch my head, just there at the very spot and I can, whenever I want to, relive that moment.

So many times I do.

'Get them.' Hugh said, and I would have, except that little bit of tin cost more than a hundred dollars and, though that usually wouldn't have stopped me, I wasn't about to have my card declined in front of him.

I put them back.

'Nope.' I gave him a smile. 'Gotta stop the impulse

spending.'

We had lunch.

Out on the pavement and I can't remember what we ate, I just remember being happy. Actually, I can remember: I had Caesar salad because it was the lowest carb thing I could find. We drank water and I *do* remember not giving it a thought.

I was just thirsty.

And happy.

He went to the loo and I chatted to a girl at the next table, just chatted away. Hugh was gone for ages and I was glad I hadn't demanded Dan from the universe, because I would have been worried about how long he was taking.

Do I go on about the universe too much? I don't know, but what I do know is that something *was* looking out for me, helping me to be my best, not to **** this up as I usually do. You see, we walked on the beach, we went for another coffee and by that time it was evening and we went home and he gave me a present.

Those Russian dolls.

I held them in my palm, and it was the nicest thing he could have done for me.

They are absolutely my favourite thing and I've just stopped to look at them now. I've just stopped to take them apart and then put them all back together again and I can still feel the wonder I felt on that day.

He was the only man who had bought something for me, I mean something truly special. Something beautiful, something thoughtful, something just for me.

Available at millsandboon.co.uk